"Who shall I say is calling, please?"

Sara simply gave her name. A moment later, the voice came back to say, "Mr. Dryden has told me to inform you he is out, Miss Peterson."

"Peters," Sara corrected automatically. "In that case, please tell Mr. Dryden I'll have to keep ringing until I find him in."

Her mind was drifting when a different voice muttered, "All right, Miss Peterson, if you insist—"

"Peters," Sara inserted, but that was all she was allowed to get in.

"Miss whatever-your-name-is, then, I'm going to have to be blunt. Granted I may have enjoyed sleeping with you. To be frank, I don't really remember. But I have no desire to repeat the experience, so if you could stop calling, I'd be grateful. I trust I've made myself clear?"

Scottish-born **ALISON FRASER** presently lives in Hertfordshire, England, with her husband and three dogs. After specializing in English and Social Sciences at Aberdeen University, she taught mathematics at London and Birmingham schools for five years, then was a computer programmer for five years for a Midlands engineering firm. Her first book, written as relaxation from work, was not publishable, but she persisted. Though she says writing doesn't come easily, she enjoys the idea of people gaining pleasure from her books. Reading, bridge and backgammon are among her other interests.

Books by Alison Fraser

HARLEQUIN PRESENTS

Don't miss any of our special offers. Write to us at the following address for information on our newest releases.

Harlequin Reader Service
P.O. Box 1397, Buffalo, NY 14240
Canadian address: P.O. Box 603,
Fort Erie, Ont. L2A 5X3

ALISON FRASER

time to let go

Harlequin Books

TORONTO • NEW YORK • LONDON
AMSTERDAM • PARIS • SYDNEY • HAMBURG
STOCKHOLM • ATHENS • TOKYO • MILAN

Harlequin Presents first edition January 1992
ISBN 0-373-11425-7

Original hardcover edition published in 1990
by Mills & Boon Limited

TIME TO LET GO

CHAPTER ONE

SARA PETERS paused at the top of the police station steps. The noise from inside was discouraging. It sounded worse than the usual Saturday night chaos, but then Christmas was only a few days away.

Steeling herself, she walked through the glass doors to be greeted by an out-of-tune rendition of 'I Belong to Glasgow'. It came from a drunk that two constables were attempting to book in. She waited patiently while the desk sergeant attempted to elicit name as well as birthplace from the nostalgic Scot.

'And how's my favourite social worker?' Sergeant Cotton asked when he finally turned to her.

Sara gave him a sceptical look. She was quite aware that he didn't wholeheartedly approve of her work; in some ways he felt it undermined his. But they were still on good terms and she replied pleasantly enough, 'Not so bad, Sarge. I see you're busy.'

'Busy!' He grunted at the understatement. 'Not ten yet and every cell's full. God knows what we're going to do when the pubs shut. Whoever said this was the season of goodwill?'

'I know what you mean.' Sara echoed his gloomy tone. She too saw a bleaker side to the Christmas festivities— kids neglected and mistreated the rest of the year often fared worse during this period.

'Getting you down, love?' the sergeant asked.

Sara shrugged, an acceptance of the inevitable. After seven years with Fulham Social Services, it was hard not to be pessimistic. She came to the point of her visit. 'So where's your waif and stray?'

5

'In one of the interview rooms—*away from this bedlam*!' The sergeant pitched his voice above the increasing hubbub.

'A runaway?' Sara enquired, checking the information supplied her over the telephone.

'It's possible. We picked him up about two hours ago in Bishop's Park.'

'What was he up to?'

'Oh, nothing criminal as far as we know,' the sergeant reassured. 'It was just his manner. Made the patrolmen wonder if he was a runner, especially when he wouldn't give his name or address.'

'What's he like?' Sara pursued.

'Surly and uncommunicative!'

'Tell me something new, Sarge,' she laughed, used to difficult children.

'Not your run-of-the-mill tearaway, though,' he added.

'In what way?'

'You'll see, love...you'll see.'

The sergeant escorted Sara down a corridor to the end interview room. She paused at the window inset in the door and saw what he'd meant the moment she took stock of the boy seated at a table, determinedly ignoring the WPC supervising him.

Sara's normal waifs were often unattractive children, their defiance a pathetic sight. But, in this boy, the sulkiness about his eyes and mouth did not detract from a face that was already strikingly handsome.

'Good-looking lad,' the sergeant echoed her thoughts. 'That's why we took him off the streets. Some funny people about.'

'Yes.' Sara understood the last comment only too well. 'Has he said anything at all?'

'One of the patrolmen said he muttered something like "Neville will kill me", before clamming up altogether,' Sergeant Cotton relayed.

'Neville?'

'Search me, love.'

The sergeant hunched his shoulders, before pushing open the door for Sara and signalling the woman constable to come away with him.

Left alone with the boy, Sara took the chair opposite. He slid her a surreptitious glance, then returned to staring at the table-top.

She bided her time, eyeing him thoughtfully as she confirmed her first opinion. He was a very attractive boy, with well-cut features and straight black hair that fell across his forehead in a fringe.

She switched her appraisal to his clothes. The grey jacket he was wearing looked tailored, and his shirt was still crisply white. Its open neck suggested a tie had been contemptuously pocketed, but from his state of cleanliness she doubted he'd been sleeping rough.

Initial assessment made, Sara continued to wait until finally her patience was rewarded when his ran out.

'Are you a lady detective?' Sharply intelligent blue eyes were fixed on her face.

She was careful to hide any satisfaction. He might not have responded to police questioning, but it was a rare child who could stand total silence for long.

'No,' she replied simply.

He frowned at the brevity of her answer. 'Then who are you?'

'My name's Mrs Peters. I'm a social worker,' she identified herself to the boy, then waited once more for him to take the initiative.

From their first word exchange, she'd noted the boy was well-spoken, with no regional accent to help trace his home area. Also, from the quality of his uniform, he probably attended a private school. The badge on his blazer pocket certainly wasn't familiar to her.

'Shouldn't you be asking me questions?' he eventually prompted.

'Are you going to answer them?' Again Sara's tone was deliberately casual.

It elicited a grudging, 'I might.'

'OK. What's your name?' she asked.

After a lengthy pause he replied, 'Walter.'

Sara's gaze widened slightly behind her heavy-framed spectacles. The boy was no more called Walter than she was. Used to lies, what surprised her was his quaint choice of alias.

'All right, *Walter*,' she played along, but his sharp glance recognised the irony in her voice, 'would you like to tell me where you live?'

'London,' he volunteered with an amused note to his voice.

'Well, that narrows things down considerably.' Sara smiled, recognising the humour. 'I don't suppose you'd like to pinpoint it more exactly? Inner London? Outer London? Or maybe London, Ontario?'

He gave her a look as if he doubted there was a London, Ontario, but allowed himself a small grin. 'Inner London.' It was his turn to play along. Not that his answer told her much. Inner London was a densely populated area.

'Fulham?' Her suggestion drew a shake of the head, so Sara added, 'In that case, what were you doing in Bishop's Park?'

'Nothing. Just walking around.'

'Why there?'

'You wouldn't believe me,' the boy said, more amused than wary.

'Try me.' Sara shrugged back.

'All right. Did you ever see the film *The Omen*?' she was asked, and at her puzzled nod he explained, 'Well, Bishop's Park is where they filmed the scene with the devil chasing the priest, and the church at the bottom is where the spire broke off and speared him to death.'

'*Really.*' Sara was suitably impressed by this gruesome piece of information. 'Where did you learn that? In a magazine?'

'No, Neville told me when it was on TV,' the boy replied.

'Neville?' She queried the name he'd already mentioned to the police, but his eyes became guarded again.

'A schoolfriend,' he eventually muttered—plainly lie number two. 'Anyway, I wasn't doing anything wrong, so I don't see that the police have any reason to hold me. They haven't even read me my rights.'

Sara stifled an impulse to laugh. 'Cops and robbers' films had a lot to answer for. She had the feeling young 'Walter' was a cinema-lover.

'They only do that when they're going to charge you with something,' she told him seriously, 'and they have no intention of doing that. So if that's what's stopping you giving me your address, I promise to take you home myself and explain things to your parents.'

He considered her offer for a long moment before announcing, 'I haven't any.'

'Any what?' Sara had lost the thread of the conversation.

'Parents. I'm an orphan,' he claimed, and his jaw jutted pugnaciously at Sara's doubting glance.

Was he lying again? He didn't look like her idea of an orphan, but then she was more familiar with kids who lived in children's homes where budgets didn't stretch to hand-made school uniforms. If he was an orphan, he had a fairy godmother or father somewhere in the background.

'What happened to them?' she said and he took his time in replying, as though he was making up a story.

She suspected he was when he announced, 'My mother killed herself.'

Showing no reaction, she confined herself to asking, 'And your father?'

'I don't have one. I'm a bastard,' he replied, eyes watching for the effect.

Sara could have told him she had long since ceased to be shocked by anything. However, she decided the boy had problems. Even if he was lying, those were disturbing lies to make up.

'So who looks after you?' she pursued.

'No one. I look after myself,' he said with the same uncaring air.

And maybe she was growing cynical in her old age but Sara had the feeling he was playing some character he had seen in a film. 'How old are you?' she asked next, and, at his silence, deliberately underestimated, 'Eleven?'

'Thirteen,' he corrected on an indignant note.

Then she tried rephrasing her earlier question. 'So, who do you live with?'

'Nobody,' he insisted stubbornly, dropping his eyes from hers.

Reluctantly Sara changed tack. 'Could you turn out your pockets for me, please?'

'Why?' he retorted, tone resentful.

'Just do it, mm?' she said, not unpleasantly, and grimaced as he muttered something about invasion of privacy and social worker brutality.

He watched with sullen eyes as she sorted through the contents of his pockets. She unfolded a scribbled note. It said, 'An early Christmas present, squirt. Consider it a bribe... Regards, N.'

Attached to the note were five ten-pound postal orders.

'Who's N?' she asked, and, at his blank look, suggested, 'Neville?'

'Maybe,' he conceded.

Sara pulled a slight face. If it was Neville, he certainly wasn't the schoolfriend claimed. Not giving fifty-pound Christmas gifts, at any rate.

'A bribe for what?' she pursued.

But the boy had clammed up again and gone back to admiring the table. She sorted through the rest of his possessions, and, picking up a used train ticket and crumpled school tie, she rose from the table.

'Where are you going?' he demanded.

She paused at the door, saying, 'To make a phone call.'

'You're coming back?' he added quickly.

And Sara thought, Poor kid, as she sensed that under the blasé act he was just a little scared. She gave a re-assuring nod, before going in search of a telephone.

She reappeared some ten minutes later, but the relief in the boy's eyes faded rapidly as she resumed, 'Listen, Walter, sooner or later we are going to have to notify whoever's responsible for your welfare. Now, I know you attend St Bartholomew's, near Canterbury, and I could call the school, but I prefer you told me about yourself voluntarily.'

'How did you find out about St Bart's?' he demanded, too amazed to deny it.

'Well, your train ticket revealed you'd travelled up from Kent,' she explained. 'The rest was luck. I have a cousin who's a master at a public school down there. When I described your tie and blazer to him, he came up with St Bartholomew's.'

'You sure you're not with the police?' the boy said, and his sour tone told her it wasn't meant as a compliment.

'OK, it was a little sneaky of me,' she conceded. 'But you must realise we'll find out about you in the end.'

'I suppose,' he agreed reluctantly.

'So, if there's a reason you're scared to go home, tell me. I'm not saying I can bail you out of any trouble you're in, but I'll try,' Sara promised quietly, then held the testing stare she was given. His trust was slow to come and went no further than a cautious nod. Tentatively she suggested, 'Maybe we could start with your name. It's not Walter, is it?'

It proved a good start for, with a small smile, he admitted, 'No, it's Scott,' and, seeing his cleverness had gone unappreciated, added, 'Walter...Scott—get it?'

Sara had to smile in return. 'I thought it a strange choice of alias. So who's Neville...Neville Chamberlain, perhaps?'

'Oh, no, Neville is Neville—and boy, is he going to be mad! You see he's really my... my guardian, sort of,' the boy said after some hesitation. 'And, well, when school broke up today...'

'You should have been home hours ago,' Sara suggested when he trailed off.

But he shook his head. 'Not exactly. To be honest, I'm meant to go to my Aunt Pauline's in Hastings for Christmas. The bribe was for good behaviour.'

'But you decided to come up to London instead.' This time Sara drew a nod, and she gently prompted, 'Do you think you could give me your aunt's telephone number? She's going to be terribly worried by this time.'

'Not her! She only has me because Neville pays her to,' he claimed scornfully. 'She's a real mercenary bitch.'

Now Sara was disconcerted, not so much at his words but by the adult cynicism behind them.

Noticing her frown, he added defensively, 'That's what Neville calls her,' as though it justified his doing so.

Bully for Neville, Sara thought sourly, wondering what kind of man packed a kid off to his aunt's, first making it clear he was only taken on sufferance.

'Anyway, she's not expecting me any more,' the boy went on, reddening as he confessed, 'You see, I got one of the seniors to—um—send her a telemessage. It was supposed to be from Neville, saying he'd changed his mind about having me for Christmas.'

'So that's why you've travelled up to London? To stay with this Neville?'

'Yes, only...'

'Only he doesn't know it yet,' Sara concluded drily, and received a sheepish grin in reply. 'Why was he sending you to your aunt's in the first place?' she added, concerned over the reception he might expect.

'It's not that he doesn't want me,' the boy claimed with almost angry conviction. 'It's just that his mother is descending on him for a couple of weeks and she *loathes* me.'

Again he gave the impression he was quoting the man, and Sara thought what a really sweet character this Neville sounded. 'But you'd still prefer to stay with him?' she said in a doubtful tone.

'Oh, yes, he's much better fun than Aunt Pauline,' Scott declared positively before his grin switched to a grimace as he qualified, 'Apart from when he's in a bad mood, that is.'

'What happens then?' Sara prompted.

'Well, if you're smart, you make yourself scarce,' the boy confided with a shaky laugh.

Sara frowned as she imagined what might happen when he wasn't smart enough to avoid his guardian's temper. Considering all too familiar possibilities, she warned herself not to jump to conclusions. 'How do you believe he will react to the present situation?' she asked carefully.

After a moment's thought, his mouth pulled down at the corners. 'I suppose he's not going to be very pleased about the telemessage.'

'No,' she agreed, 'I think that's a fair assumption.'

'But he'll be OK after he's yelled a bit,' the boy decided more optimistically.

'Are you sure?'

'Fairly. I mean he likes having me around. He said so. More than *her* at any rate.'

'Her?' Sara repeated the word laden with derision.

'His mother.'

'What's she like?'

'Acts as though she's in her twenties, dresses like she's in her thirties, and looks on the wrong side of seventy,' the boy said as if from memory.

'Is that Neville's opinion?' Sara enquired astutely, and got her answer in a quick blush. Obviously the man didn't believe in toning down his conversation for the boy. 'All right, how about if I telephone him to come and collect you?'

'OK. Perhaps you'll be able to persuade him not to be too mad.' He gave Sara a hopeful look.

'I wouldn't count on it,' she warned, 'but I'll do my best.'

'He likes women,' the boy added.

Sara wasn't too sure how to respond to the confidence. She already had a fair idea what form that 'liking' took. She confined herself to asking for his guardian's full name and telephone number.

The boy scribbled both on a scrap of paper, and, when he handed it over, peered at her as if waiting for some reaction.

'I hope you're not leading me up the garden path,' she said, catching that odd look.

'No, of course not!' he denied on an indignant note. 'I just thought... well, that you might have heard of Neville.'

'Why?' Sara asked, but the hunch of his shoulders dismissed whatever reason he had, and she didn't pursue it.

Later she wished she had. At least she might have had some warning what to expect when she dialled the number from the privacy of the sergeant's office.

The telephone was answered immediately and a toneless voice confirmed, 'Yes, this is Mr Neville Dryden's residence. Who shall I say is calling, please?'

Sara simply gave her name, not wanting to cause alarm by revealing her identity to a third party.

A minute later the same voice came back to relay, 'I'm afraid Mr Dryden has told me to inform you he is out, Miss Peterson.'

'Peters,' Sara corrected automatically before the man-servant's words sank in. She repeated slowly, 'He's *told* you to say he's out?'

'Yes,' the voice on the other end confirmed without embarrassment.

It was certainly one way of discouraging unwanted callers, Sara thought, as she realised the rudeness was quite deliberate. 'In that case,' she replied with laudable restraint, 'could you please go and tell Mr Dryden I'll have to keep ringing until I find him in?'

'Very well, miss,' the man agreed, and Sara was again left waiting on the line.

In fact she was kept waiting so long, her mind was drifting when a different voice muttered in her ear, 'All right, Miss Peterson, if you insist——'

'Peters,' Sara inserted, but that was all she was al-lowed to get in.

'Miss whatever-your-name-is, then. I can see I'm going to have to be blunt,' the voice informed her, then con-tinued in a languid drawl, 'Granted, I may have enjoyed sleeping with you. To be frank, I don't really remember. But I have no desire to repeat the experience, so if you could stop calling I'd be grateful. My ego certainly doesn't need it and I don't believe it can be doing much for yours, either... I trust I've made myself clear?'

Sara wasn't capable of a coherent answer but her speechless gasp was taken for one. This time she was left holding a dead line.

She was still holding it when the sergeant returned to ask, 'Did you get through?'

'Yes and no,' she said, slowly coming out of her daze. 'I talked to the man—or, at least, he talked to me. He seemed to think I was somebody else.'

'Who, exactly?' the sergeant quizzed, intrigued by the colour fanning her cheeks.

'It doesn't matter.' Sara decided against passing on the content of the brief conversation. She had a suspicion the sergeant would find it amusing and she might direct her temper at the wrong man. 'I think you'd better telephone him.'

'If you want, but getting a call from the police often gives people a few anxious moments.'

'Don't worry—he'll survive. Here...' She handed him the slip of paper with the number and the sergeant's eyebrows shot up.

'Well, well! You kept quiet about that.'

'What?' Sara stared at him blankly.

'Who the laddie's guardian is. Neville Dryden, no less!' he said, visibly impressed, but her blank look persisted. 'The actor, love? *Deadly Games*, *A State of Mind*, *The Harrison Scandal*... Don't you watch telly?' the sergeant finally asked when she showed no recognition of the plays named.

'Not much.' Sara preferred reading.

'Films, then?' She shook her head and he gave her a look that questioned where she'd been for the last decade. 'He's been a household name for years. Often in the papers, and not just for his acting, if you know what I mean.'

'I can guess,' Sara said, tight-lipped.

'Wait till I tell the wife. She's a big fan—along with most of the ladies, I believe,' he chuckled, then, catching Sara's singularly unamused expression, stressed, 'Don't get me wrong. He's more than just a pretty face. Very good actor in my opin——'

'Yes, Sarge,' Sara cut in, having already heard enough about the illustrious Neville Dryden, and pointedly held out the receiver. 'Well, why don't you give him a call? I'm sure he'll be glad to hear your opinion. And while you're at it, perhaps you could mention the boy—in passing, as it were?'

'Now, I wonder what he said to ruffle your normally calm feathers, Mrs Peters,' the sergeant mused, before raising his hands at the glare he received. 'All right, all right, I'll phone. But you are going to stick around till he shows up?'

Sara nodded curtly, knowing she should even if she had no wish to meet the man. It wasn't that she had been embarrassed by the things he'd said over the phone. Obviously they'd not been intended for her and she'd heard more offensive things in the course of her work. Social workers weren't everybody's favourite people.

No, it was anger she was feeling, stirred by the drawling arrogance of the man. What were his words? He may have enjoyed sleeping with her but he really couldn't remember!

And there was the boy. On the evidence so far, she did not consider Neville Dryden ideal guardian material.

That Scott did think a lot of him was implicit in the eager way he asked on her return, 'What did Neville say? Did he say I could stay? You didn't tell him I was in trouble, did you?'

'I didn't actually speak to him,' she said, almost truthfully considering how brief her contribution to the conversation had been. 'The sergeant's calling him now.'

His mouth took on a sulky curve. 'I thought you were going to put a word in for me.'

'I said I'd *try*,' Sara reminded, 'and I will.'

She didn't go further. She had a feeling the chances of her influencing Mr Neville Dryden were very slim. She felt no more hopeful when the sergeant popped his head round the door to tell them the man was on his way.

The boy must have sensed her doubts, as he said, 'Neville can be a bit funny when he wants, but he's OK underneath. He just plays up to it—his image, I mean. He's an actor, you know.'

'Yes, the sergeant told me.'

'Anyway, he hates people fawning over him simply because he's famous, so sometimes he can be sort of awkward.'

'Really.' Sara gathered she was being coached on how to handle the man who was beginning to sound more obnoxious with each reference. 'Well, don't worry. I'll restrain any fawning urges that come over me.'

The boy's eyes narrowed on her. 'Are you sending me up?'

'A little,' she admitted.

Catching on, he said with emphasis, 'I didn't mean *you* would fawn or anything. It's only... well, women tend to throw themselves at him. But of course you're not likely to, are you?'

'Not a chance,' Sara confirmed and drew a nod of approval.

'For one thing,' he continued humorously, 'you're about ten times smarter than most of the women he goes out with.'

'Thank you.' She smiled in response.

'And for another, you're married,' he added in the same vein, only this time Sara's face sobered. 'Did I say something wrong?'

'No.' She shook her head, as much at herself as the boy. Was she still so sensitive?

'I'm not putting you off him, am I?' he said, frowning.

'No,' Sara repeated, which was not exactly a lie—she had already been 'off him' before the boy had started.

'Good.' He was mistakenly satisfied with her reply. 'It's just that some people misunderstand him.'

'Oh,' Sara murmured non-committally. Personally she felt she'd understood the man only too well.

'But you'll probably like him,' the boy declared, eyes gravely considering the possibility.

Not sharing his optimism, Sara made no comment. Most of the time she tried to reserve judgement on people, but she had a premonition that here was one fan club she wasn't about to join.

CHAPTER TWO

SARA'S premonition proved correct. Neville Dryden appeared half an hour later, resplendent in evening suit beneath a cashmere overcoat, and he had her hackles rising from the moment the sergeant introduced them.

This time it wasn't at what he said, but how he looked at her—amused, knowing, slightly disdainful—as he marked her off as another conquest.

Admittedly she had been staring at him rather hard. She imagined he was used to that, with his tall, powerful build and his dark, dramatic looks. But it was pure conceit to assume she'd been bowled over by his presence. If he was striking, in a cold, arrogant sort of way, it was his remarkable likeness to Scott that had actually caught her attention.

'I'll leave you to it, then,' Sergeant Cotton said. 'And, Mr Dryden, thanks for the autograph. My wife will be tickled pink.'

'A pleasure.' The actor smiled as the sergeant reluctantly departed.

A charming, meaningless smile, Sara thought when it was turned on her, and, lips tightening fractionally, she said, 'Please take a seat, Mr Dryden.'

He hesitated, glanced round the barely furnished room once and gave what sounded like a resigned sigh before sitting down at the table. Sara noted each gesture with mounting irritation.

She'd arranged for Scott to have tea in the police canteen while she interviewed the man separately, but now she found herself lost for a suitable opening.

20

He, on the other hand, looked completely at ease, drawing out a gold case to offer her a cigarette. They were an unusual brand, black with a gold filter, and Sara shook her head, deciding not to risk a coughing fit if they proved too strong.

'I suppose I should really apologise . . .' he began after lighting one for himself.

Not unnaturally, Sara waited for him to say more. When he failed to, she eventually realised that that was it—her apology. Or the nearest she was going to get in that amused drawl of his.

And there was absolutely nothing apologetic in the smile flashed at her. Again full of practised charm, it antagonised Sara more and made her wonder what re-action he expected. She had a feeling the actor didn't object to fawning as much as the boy had claimed.

'If you're referring to our telephone conversation earlier, there's no need. I gathered you'd mistaken me for someone else,' she said, her voice cool with indifference.

Indifference, however, was not something Neville Dryden was in the habit of encountering. It made him sit up slightly, and drop his languid air as he appraised the woman across the table from him.

Aware of his scrutiny, Sara did not flatter herself she was going to come out of it favourably. Even if heavy-framed glasses and a serviceable bun had not been con-cealing wide-set dark brown eyes and the rich chestnut of her hair, she doubted she would be considered at-tractive by this man's standards. Her face was stamped with intelligence rather than any great beauty.

But Sara cared little about his opinion. In fact, she hoped that if he saw her as plain, it might mean he'd start treating the situation with some vestige of seriousness.

It didn't. When he'd finished his appraisal, he drawled back, 'Yes, well, I must say it's good of you to be so understanding, Miss Peterson. But just for the record, I'm sure if we had—um—met, I would certainly have remembered you.'

God, he's awful, Sara groaned silently at what was presumably intended as a compliment. Not only did he seem incapable of switching off the charm, he hadn't even the decency to get her name right.

'It's Peters, Mrs,' she corrected flatly.

'Sorry, Peters . . . *Mrs*,' he repeated, a mocking edge now to his voice.

Her lack of personal interest in him at last seemed to be penetrating. She emphasised it by continuing, 'If we could talk about the boy, Mr Dryden?'

'If we must,' he said on a patently bored note, reinforced by his tapping the rim of the ashtray with his cigarette. 'So where is Superbrat? You haven't locked him in a cell, have you? I know he's a pain, but really . . .' He trailed off, observing the disapproval written all over Sara's face. He scarcely looked subdued, however—more satisfied, as though he'd just scored a point.

Sara found herself having to count to ten. Hardened to verbal abuse, she found this man's brand of provocation an entirely different matter.

'By Superbrat I take it you mean Walter,' she replied stiffly, then too late caught her mistake. What on earth had made her say the wrong name?

It gave him the opportunity to correct her. 'No, actually, I mean Scott. But don't be alarmed, it's probably the same boy. Black hair, blue eyes, high forehead. Handsome little devil—or so people say.'

Sara wondered why he bothered describing the boy unless it was to amuse himself at her expense. It was certainly unnecessary. No one could fail to notice that the boy was a younger edition of the man himself, right down to the groove in their cheeks when they smiled. Any differences were down to age, the lines fanning the man's eyes indicating he was nearer forty than thirty.

Guardian indeed! Sara thought scornfully, but decided not to challenge him on it. She was having enough problems steering the conversation on to a reasonable level.

'I assume Walter was a spur of the moment invention. Well, at least it shows he's vaguely literate,' Dryden continued musingly.

'Sorry?' Sara caught only the tail-end of his comment.

'Walter...Scott.' He linked the two names together, then felt it necessary to explain, 'Sir Walter Scott. Nineteenth-century novelist. Wrote the——'

'Waverley novels,' Sara cut in before he could make her out to be a complete dimwit. 'Yes, Mr Dryden, I *have* heard of him.'

Her irritation was registered with another smile which annoyed her even more, before he suddenly returned to asking, 'So where is he? Scott, I mean—not Sir Walter.'

And Sara felt that if she didn't lose her patience during this interview, she deserved sainthood.

'He's been taken to the canteen upstairs for some sandwiches,' she told him, struggling to keep her tone neutral. 'He's had nothing since breakfast at school and he's been wandering round London most of the day.'

The man's forehead creased slightly but there was no detectable concern in his comment of, 'Getting up the nerve to come home, I take it?'

And Sara's reply was pure impulse as she snapped back, 'Why? Does he need it?'

Sharp and accusing, as well as totally unprofessional! Sara realised it herself before she met the blue eyes winging back to her. Yet she wasn't quite prepared for the effect her bluntness had, as his mouth lost its amused curve and the handsome face went into rigid lines, revealing a strong will behind his dubious charm.

'I don't physically mistreat the boy, if that's what you're asking,' he stated after a long, silent stare. 'And even allowing for Scott's admittedly fertile imagination, I have difficulty believing *he* has suggested I do.'

His derisive tone implied more than that Scott suffered from a fertile imagination, and Sara was left regretting her outburst. However insufferable the man, it was not in the boy's interests to alienate him.

Backing down, she replied stiffly, 'I'm sorry if I gave you the wrong impression, Mr Dryden. As you say, Scott has in no way implied he is badly treated. In fact, he is anxious that you'll let him stay with you over Christmas.'

'Is that so?' he said without any apparent interest, then showed he was aware of how forced her apology had been by adding, 'Well, there's no accounting for taste...is there, Miss—*Mrs* Peters?'

Sara was sorely tempted to be just as frank and agree. Why anyone would actively seek out this man's company was almost beyond comprehension. She could only wonder what Scott's aunt was like if he preferred this sarcastic brute.

Taking a deep breath, she tried again. 'Look, Mr Dryden, I understand you might resent my interference——'

'You do?' he inserted with heavy irony.

'*However,*' she continued through gritted teeth, 'you at least must see that we are concerned with Scott's welfare.'

'Oh, at least,' he mocked her less than diplomatic phrasing, before conceding, 'All right, what do you want to know?'

He seemed ready to co-operate, but, when he lounged back in his chair and crossed his arms, he was wearing an expression of such bored resignation that Sara asked herself why she was bothering. Nothing would make this man do what he didn't want to, and his very uninterest suggested Scott would be on a train to his aunt's in Hastings by morning. Still, she had to go through the motions.

'I believe you're Scott's guardian?' She received a brief nod. 'Are you a relative?'

She half anticipated an outright denial, but he slanted his head as though to draw attention to his likeness to Scott. 'What do you think?'

Taking it as another 'yes', Sara added, 'And his mother?'

'She's dead,' he said, confirming, in part, what Scott had told her.

Perhaps the rest was also true—that his mother had committed suicide. But she decided against delving further in case Scott had been dramatising.

'Is that all?' he enquired, surprised she hadn't followed it up.

'Almost, Mr Dryden.' A dry note crept into Sara's voice as she glanced at his evening clothes. 'I can see you have other plans for the evening.'

'*Had,*' he corrected blandly. 'A rather lovely blonde, to be precise, but don't let it worry you.'

'I won't,' Sara muttered, not intending the comment for his ears.

That he did catch it became evident from the raising of his dark eyebrows, followed by a low, amused laugh. Then he flicked back a starched white cuff to consult the gold watch on his wrist. 'Nevertheless, as she's waiting in the car, perhaps we could wrap this up?'

The arrogance of it, close to suggesting she was prolonging the interview, finally proved too much for Sara's temper.

'Mr Dryden, for all I care, you can go take a run——' she began furiously, only to be cut short by a knock on the door and the reappearance of the WPC.

Of course Neville Dryden must have gathered her general sentiments. A glance told her that. He was smirking as if he'd personally arranged the interruption.

Then he tried the devastating smile on the young policewoman, and the girl's face suffused with colour—a shy, pleased pink.

So that's how I was meant to react, Sara thought. It was small wonder the man was unbearably conceited.

The WPC sounded almost breathless as she explained that she'd brought Scott back. Hiding exasperation, Sara murmured a bare thanks and asked her to send him in from the corridor.

The boy entered cautiously, eyes going to the man. Sara read fear in his expression as he waited judgement, a fear she shared when Neville Dryden glowered back at him. With his dark brows drawn in a thunderous line, he couldn't have looked more malevolent if he'd tried.

Which made it baffling when the boy's lips twitched into a smile, as he appealed, 'You mad, Neville?'

'Seething,' his guardian confirmed, but in his usual languid drawl. 'In fact, I'm considering taking a stick to you when we get home.'

'You wouldn't!' Scott countered, quite certain he was being teased.

'Want to bet?' the man challenged before shooting Sara a look that caught the full force of her hostility. Then, as if it alone made him reconsider, he sighed, 'No, perhaps not. I wouldn't like Mrs Peters here to get the wrong idea.'

Wouldn't he, though? Sara fumed, wise to the charade just acted out for her benefit. It was obvious from Scott's grin, matching the man's, that there was not the remotest possibility of physical punishment being administered.

'She said she'd put in a word for me,' he claimed, now confident of Neville's good mood and mistakenly attributing it to Sara's powers of persuasion.

'She did,' Dryden murmured, a statement for the boy, but a mocking brow was lifted in Sara's direction.

Lips tightening, she understood the gesture only too well. What few words she had managed to put in had been treated with the same amused disdain.

'Does that mean I don't have to go to Aunt Pauline's for Christmas?' Scott pressed.

Neville Dryden's face sobered. 'Possibly, but don't think I'm going to overlook that stunt you pulled.'

'Stunt?' Scott echoed.

'I telephoned Pauline before I came here, asking why she hadn't reported you missing. Apparently *I'd* sent a message informing her of my decision to take you over Christmas.' An accusing stare was levelled on the boy.

'Oh.' His face turned a guilty pink.

'Yes ... *oh*.' The man clearly expected an explanation, but, eyes flicking to Sara, he confined himself to saying, 'We'll speak about it later.'

Scott nodded, aware he was in for an uncomfortable lecture, then, more subdued, he repeated, 'But I can stay with you over Christmas ... at least until I go skiing with the school?'

Sensing him holding his breath, Sara felt a stab of pity for the boy. His father—for that was who she assumed Neville Dryden must be—didn't seem to share his anxiety that they spend Christmas together. Not from the amount of time he took to think about it.

'I suppose I can put up with you for a week. Just remember we won't be alone, mm?' he replied, the first offhand, the last a dry warning.

Scott, however, didn't appear to be discouraged by either, coming back with a grin, 'Don't worry. I'll keep a low profile.'

A wry laugh greeted the promise. '*That*, squirt, I shall believe when I see,' Neville Dryden drawled, and a conspiratorial look passed between the two.

Sara could only guess at its meaning. She recalled Scott's mentioning that Neville Dryden's mother—his grandmother—did not like him, but she had difficulty accepting that the boy was shunted elsewhere because of it. Wasn't it perhaps more likely that the 'rather lovely blonde' waiting in the car was the real reason?

Well, whichever was true, Scott had what he wanted. From his glowing face, it was painfully obvious that he was grateful for any attention, however offhand.

The same could not be said for Sara. When the man switched his smile to her, she remained impassive, and gradually the smile turned to a look of puzzlement.

Why he should be puzzled, Sara could not understand. She did not know yet that Neville Dryden was used to those around him putting up with, then forgiving his awkward moods. She just thought the actor must be monumentally conceited to expect other than dislike after his earlier 'performance'.

Indeed, her rising to put on her coat attracted more of his drawling sarcasm. 'Dare I take it that we are free to go?'

It took her some seconds to think of a reply rude enough to match his question, and by that time she'd intercepted the boy's pleading glance.

'Naturally,' she said with commendable restraint. 'Scott hasn't done anything wrong.'

There was nothing pointed about the remark but the man read it that way, responding drily, 'Well, I'm glad one of us meets with your approval, Mrs Peters.'

'Neville, *don't*!' Scott muttered in a low voice, and was shot a look of total surprise for it.

But if Dryden was even more unused to criticism from the boy, he accepted it with a shrug. 'Whatever you say, squirt. Mrs Peters realises I was joking.'

Was he? Sara didn't think so. If she forced a weak smile, it was solely for Scott's benefit. And, deciding she'd had enough of his father, she led the way out to the reception area.

'Everything sorted out?' Sergeant Cotton asked when he spotted them.

The question was directed at Sara, but she was so slow in replying that Neville Dryden spoke for her.

'Yes, thank you, Sergeant. And, on Scott's behalf, I'd like to apologise for any waste of your time. I can see you're busy.'

'Just a normal Saturday night, sir,' the sergeant remarked on the chaos round them. 'No need to apologise. Glad to be of service. That's what we're here for.'

The sergeant's cheeriness was a marked contrast to his mood when Sara had first arrived, and, having heard his opinion on the current lack of parental supervision, she thought he was being unusually generous. But then Neville Dryden *was* a celebrity.

'Anyway, it's Sara who deserves any credit,' the sergeant continued, possibly misreading her exasperated look.

'Sara?' Neville Dryden echoed.

'Mrs Peters here,' the sergeant relayed. 'Got a way with kids, she has. Couldn't get a word out of the lad before she——'

'Sarge,' Sara interrupted, not wanting her virtues extolled, particularly in front of their current audience. 'Sorry to cut in, but I'd better be going before I miss my bus.'

She gave a brief nod to Neville Dryden, a noticeably warmer smile to Scott, and said a hasty goodnight to the sergeant before he could think too much about her excuse.

She knew it was a lame one. That was confirmed later as she waited in the pouring rain at a stop on Fulham Palace Road. She hadn't a clue if the next bus would be along in five minutes or thirty. London buses tended to operate to an erratic timetable.

She was already drenched after the short walk from the police station and, while the rain beat relentlessly down, she began to blame Neville Dryden for her misery. Perverse logic, perhaps, but if she hadn't been so anxious to get away from him, the sergeant might have arranged a police car to drive her home. Therefore the cold she was probably catching was all his fault.

Just like everything else, she decided, absolving herself over the way she'd handled him—or hadn't, as the case might be. After all, how could you reason with a man like that? She only wished she had managed to tell him he could go take a running jump. If she'd the chance again, she would.

At least that was what she was telling herself the very moment a dark, sleek Daimler drew up at the bus-stop and pomped its horn. The streets were deserted on the dark, wet night, and she was vaguely alarmed until a back window slid down and Scott popped his head out.

'Would you like a lift, Mrs Peters?' he called as she approached the kerb.

'I——' She hesitated as Neville Dryden turned round in the driver's seat to give her a look that was anything but inviting. 'You may not be going my way,' she said, guessing it had been entirely Scott's idea to stop for her.

'That doesn't matter. Does it, Neville?' He checked he had approval for his generosity, but Sara had already decided she wasn't going to accept a begrudged lift.

She forced a smile for the boy. 'It's all right, Scott. A bus will be along soon. I don't mind waiting.'

'But you're awfully wet,' he pointed out.

Sara could imagine, feeling the rain dripping down her hair and face. She noticed the woman in the front passenger seat giving her the once-over before discounting her with a smug look. She didn't know whether to be amused or irritated. Even in a dry state, she knew she'd never be competition for this glamorous blonde— nor would she want to be, considering the prize. He, too, seemed to be finding something to smirk at, as he watched her searching for excuses.

'It's very kind of you to be concerned, Scott——' She launched into another refusal but was brought to a halt by the sound of a door slamming.

She stared, open-mouthed, as Neville Dryden walked round to her side of the car, yanked open the back door, and, with the merest hint of a bow, invited her to climb in.

Still staring, Sara made no move to do so.

'I'm afraid Scott insists,' he drawled, the mockery in his eyes making it clear that he, personally, couldn't care less if she drowned in the downpour.

Sara swore to herself she wasn't going to accept the lift. Not even if they stood there the rest of the night. Which didn't seem likely when Dryden was rapidly becoming as wet as she was.

Yet seconds mounted to a full minute as their eyes met and locked and he continued to hold the door open for her, looking infuriatingly calm, being infuriatingly stubborn, until Sara realised he *was* quite prepared to stand there all night.

The man was mad!

'Thank you.' She climbed into the car, told herself she'd really won—a victory of her common sense over his insanity—and ignored Scott's grin, which saw it differently.

'Where to?' Dryden threw over his shoulder when he'd settled back in the driver's seat.

'Upper Richmond Road,' she said shortly.

'Richmond?' He turned to face her. 'Then I'm sure you'll be relieved to know we *are* going your way, Mrs Peters. What a pity you didn't say so before. It might have saved us some trouble.'

His tone was pure sarcasm and Sara gave serious thought to jumping out of the car. But before she could, he'd turned round again and started the car. Resigned, she leaned back in her seat, and received another of those apologetic glances from Scott. Angry though she was, she returned it with a shrug and a smile. The boy could hardly be held responsible for the man's behaviour.

He didn't even have the basic good manners to introduce her to his female companion and, as they headed towards Putney Bridge, the blonde herself whispered, 'Who's she?'

It was a stage whisper and would have carried across a thirty-foot room, far less to the back of a car.

'Nobody.' Dryden's dismissal was lower but still audible.

Sara scowled at his back and then tried to divorce herself from her surroundings. It was not easy. The blonde went on talking, regardless of the fact that every word of her conversation could be heard.

'Nev, darling,' she began tentatively, and Sara could have sworn Scott beside her groaned, either at the simpering tone or the abbreviation of Dryden's Christian name.

Both made Sara cringe.

'Yes?' In contrast, the man's tone was curt.

The blonde didn't appear to notice. 'I was thinking— well, you don't *have* to take me home, do you?'

There was a long moment's silence before Neville Dryden treated the question quite literally. 'No, but it's a long walk from here to Wimbledon. I wouldn't like you to get wet, Janey.'

Listening in spite of herself, Sara had to strain to catch his words but she still managed to detect the warning note in them.

Janey was oblivious, giggling, 'You're such a tease, darling. You know perfectly well I meant that——'

'Yes!' was almost snapped before she could be more explicit.

'Then why not?' Janey continued, undaunted. 'I could come back with you to the house, and after you tuck the boy up in bed we could carry on where——'

'Janey!' It was now a low, harsh command to shut up.

Rather late, for Sara had a fair idea of what the blonde had been about to suggest in her seductive purr. And Scott, several years past the tucking-up stage, also seemed wise to it. Far too wise, Sara thought, as she glanced sideways and he rolled his eyes in despair at his guardian's latest choice in girlfriends.

Janey certainly went out of her way to support the boy's claim that Dryden had a preference for stupid women. After twenty seconds' offended silence, she sniffed at him, 'You were keen enough earlier. I don't know why you're being like this.'

'No? I suppose it's too much to hope that you know the expression, little pitchers have big ears?' he asked drily, and he must have made some gesture towards the back of the car because Janey looked round. But his reference to an avidly listening Scott was plainly lost on her as it was Sara she awarded a rude, somewhat vacant stare.

And, with little confidence his subtlety would be appreciated, Neville Dryden switched to enquiring directions of Sara. The rain had suddenly stopped, but her request to be dropped at a junction on the main road was ignored. He insisted on delivering her to her doorstep, or as near as he could get in the narrow road of Victorian houses.

She thought he was taking courtesy too far, however, when he parked the car and said, 'Escort Mrs Peters to her door, Scott.'

'There's no need,' she assured, but was again overruled.

'Scott!' he prompted, and the boy didn't wait for another telling to scramble out of the car.

Sara scrambled out after him, anxious to get away, but, as she reached the pavement, the driver's window slid down with a soft, automatic purr.

'Mrs Peters?' His voice brought her to a halt beside his door.

'Yes?' Their eyes met once more, only this time there was no animosity in the look they exchanged.

For a brief instant, Sara thought she saw the man behind the actor—a shrewd, complex individual fronting as a careless charmer.

Then the look was gone, replaced by a smirk of a smile and a drawling, 'Do have a happy Christmas.'

He made it seem unlikely, as if he doubted her ability to enjoy herself, and Sara didn't waste breath replying. She walked away with Scott, pursued by the sound of Janey's vapid, girlish laughter.

'See what I mean?' Scott remarked the moment they were out of earshot. 'She's even dumber than the last one, and she was no Einstein. I don't know why he goes out with women like that.'

Sara felt she shouldn't be amused by this scathing dismissal, but she was. She would have been a hypocrite if she'd ticked him off for it. In the end she just said, 'She's very pretty.'

'Do you think so?' Scott evidently didn't, pulling a face.

'Not your type, eh?' she teased as they came to a halt outside her door.

'*Definitely* not,' he said with emphasis. 'I mean, what's the point of going out with someone you can't communicate with, other than on a primitive level? And, besides that, I bet her hair's dyed.'

The catty comment following the loftier sentiment made Sara laugh aloud. She couldn't help it. 'I shouldn't be encouraging you,' she said when he joined in. 'Are you sure you're only thirteen?'

Nodding, he showed he understood the question. 'Yes, but Neville says I'm rather precocious for my age.'

'For once Neville may have a point,' Sara said without thinking, then immediately wished she'd chosen her words with a bit more care.

'You didn't like him, did you?' Scott was obviously disappointed by the fact. 'I suppose he was being pretty awful to you. But he's not always like that—honest!'

Sara wondered if Neville Dryden appreciated his son's loyalty. She doubted it. He probably had difficulty recognising finer qualities in others, when he was so lacking in them himself.

'As long as he's good to you,' she murmured back.

'Oh, yes, he always has been,' Scott claimed almost proudly. 'Even when we lived in Manchester, he used to come and see me as often as he could. And, when Mum died, he stopped filming and flew all the way back from Australia.'

Sara felt a dry lump form in the back of her throat. Case-hardened by worse situations, yet she could have cried for this boy. So pathetically grateful for actions a child should have taken for granted from a father. So vulnerable to hurt from a man with a talent for inflicting it. And, though he appeared happy with the way the evening had turned out, some things still bothered her.

'Scott, you arrived in London at noon and the police picked you up about seven. Why didn't you go to Neville's house in that time?'

'I did, but his car wasn't outside and I thought his mother might be there, so I decided I'd better wait until he was home. Then, when the police stopped me in the park, I thought they thought I'd done something wrong. They started asking my name and where I lived—and, well, I couldn't risk involving Neville, could I?'

Sara had followed his logic up until the last remark. 'Why not?'

'In case of publicity, of course,' he said as if it should have been obvious. 'I know you haven't heard of him, but he's really very famous. And he wants it kept secret that I'm his—who I am,' Scott finished awkwardly, having almost revealed his true identity.

'I think I know who you are, Scott,' Sara admitted gently, thinking he might be dramatising the need for secrecy, but his alarmed look suggested otherwise. 'Don't worry, I wouldn't tell anyone, least of all the Press. I just wouldn't like you to feel you have to hide it from me. It's nothing you should be ashamed of.'

'No, Neville says that. It's because of his mother he has to keep it quiet. She really hates me.'

'Are you sure?' Sara wondered if he wasn't exaggerating his grandmother's dislike.

He gave a very positive nod. 'You can understand it, sort of.'

'I can't.' Sara smiled. For all his precociousness, she found Scott very likeable. She was only sorry she couldn't help him in some way. 'I'd better let you go. He'll be waiting for you.'

'Oh, Neville won't mind,' he said confidently. 'He's probably giving her hell for going on like that, for being...indiscreet? Is that the right word?'

'It'll do,' Sara said, tone wry.

'Anyway, that's why he wanted me to walk you to your door,' Scott explained. 'So he could tell her in words of one syllable to shut up in front of me. I suppose he thinks I'm too young to understand he sleeps with his girlfriends.'

Saddened that he wasn't, Sara asked quietly, 'How do you feel about that?'

'It's his life.' Scott gave a philosophic shrug, before sighing. 'I just wish he had better taste. Sometimes I'm almost embarrassed for him.'

Sara would have laughed if the remark had come from an adult. As it was, she had to struggle to keep her face straight.

'That's him,' the boy added as a horn sounded and the Daimler appeared, turned and double-parked, opposite her gate. 'I have to go. Thanks for—um—listening, Mrs Peters. I'm sorry if I spoiled your evening.'

Sara shook her head. 'Not at all. I enjoyed meeting you, Scott. In fact, you livened up my evening.'

'Did I?' He looked pleased with himself, and surprised her by asking, 'Will I see you again?'

About to say no, something in his eyes stopped Sara. She knew she shouldn't encourage him. That was the first rule of her job: you did what you could and you tried to remain detached. But then Sara had never been very good at following rules.

'Officially, no, but if you're at a loose end in the holidays, I wouldn't object to some company.'

She made the invitation casual, perhaps too casual as he frowned and said, 'You mean it?'

She nodded back. 'I'll be away from Christmas Eve to Boxing Day, but you should find me home most other days.'

'I don't know if I'll be able to come,' Scott said after a moment's thought. 'You see, I'll be going on this skiing trip on the thirtieth.'

'That's OK—your choice.' Sara understood he didn't want to commit himself and brought the conversation to an end, saying, 'Well, have a good Christmas.'

'You too,' he replied and, with a last grin, loped off to the waiting car.

The Daimler accelerated away as she fitted her key in the front door. The spurt of speed suggested impatience. She doubted she would see the boy again. Perhaps it was for the best, but she wished she could have done more for him.

Stepping inside, she unbuttoned her coat and hung it to dry on the hall-stand. A man appeared at the top of the stairs.

'You're late. Want to come up for a nightcap?'

She shook her head. 'No, thanks, Bob. I'd fall asleep on you.'

'That bad, eh?' Bob chuckled. 'The department's got a cheek, always calling you out. What was it this time?'

Being a fellow social worker, Bob was genuinely interested, but, since renting him and his wife her upstairs rooms, Sara was careful not to presume too much on their hospitality.

'Oh, nothing special.' She shrugged. 'I'll tell you tomorrow.'

'OK.' Bob saw she was tired and wet. 'Night, Sara.'

'Night, Bob,' she echoed and unlocked her flat downstairs.

She went straight to the bedroom and stripped off her wet clothing. Then, in her dressing-gown, she returned to the living-room to light the gas heater. Unpinning her hair, she sat down on the hearthrug to dry it.

At times it was a nuisance, being long and thick, and, every so often, Kathy upstairs gently hinted that a different hairstyle and new contact lenses would improve what she termed Sara's 'self-image'.

Amused by Kathy's liberal use of psychological jargon, Sara didn't actually think her self-image was in that bad a shape, but, in a weak moment, she'd agreed to treat herself to the lenses for Christmas. Cutting her hair, however, she couldn't quite bring herself to do. She made all sorts of excuses to Kathy because she knew the other girl might not understand the real reason—that Nick had liked it long.

She raised her eyes to the wedding photograph on the mantelpiece, and looked at her younger self: hair tumbling in waves beneath the white lace of her veil, eyes bright, shining, alive with happiness. And Nick beside her, thin, clever face so solemn in comparison, even while the hand tightly gripping hers betrayed the depth of his feelings.

The boy Scott had been right. She was still married— as committed to Nick now as she had been then. Hardly a day went by when she didn't think of him. Hardly a night passed when she didn't long for him, didn't imagine his body entwined with hers in sleep. Time slipped by but the love remained, as though it were just yesterday they had last lain together, whispering in the darkness, making gentle love. It didn't matter that it had been three years—three long, lonely years.

Nick had died. But the feelings hadn't. Perhaps they never would.

CHAPTER THREE

SARA spent Christmas at Orchards, her parents' home in Kent. The house owed its name to the surrounding five acres of apple and cherry trees, and was a beautiful old building of ivy-covered walls and casement windows. It had been in her family for three generations, and its size and elegance testified to the wealth of the Summerfields. Sometimes Sara felt its very grandeur to be wrong, yet she loved this home of her childhood.

Her feelings for her father were similar—disapproval tempered by love. Charles Summerfield was an unashamedly rich stockbroker, with a gift for making money which he spent lavishly on fine living, antique collecting and, when they allowed him to, his children.

He had two: Simon, at thirty-three, already a successful surgeon and a source of pride to him; and Sara, five years younger, who rarely did anything that pleased but was dearer to him than all his possessions.

Perhaps this fondness was expressed in strange ways—an exasperated look when she turned up wearing old jeans and a disreputable sweater; a pained frown when he visited her drab terrace house in London; a doubtful understanding of why she should want to spend her life dealing in other people's misery. Yet there was no doubting the affection they had for each other.

Only once had they ever quarrelled seriously. It had concerned her husband Nick and his refusal to accept the town house bought by her father as a wedding present. Proud, stubborn Nick, who had wanted them to make their own way, and whom she had loved for that alone.

* * *

He had been a friend of her brother first—they were residents in the same London hospital—and Simon had invited him to Orchards one weekend when Sara had been home from college.

On the face of it they'd had little in common. He'd been seven years older than her, infinitely more serious in personality and from a quite different background. Brought up in Newcastle, he had spent his childhood moving between foster homes, and had struggled against the odds to make it to medical school then survive six gruelling years of study to become a doctor. It had made him aloof, at times abrupt, but his undoubted brilliance had attracted Simon Summerfield.

And Sara? Nick had never seemed aloof to her. That first meeting, they'd sat in the swing-seat in her mother's rose garden and talked for hours, about everything and nothing. He had seen Sara as she really was—an intelligent girl with a generous spirit, remarkably unspoilt by her parents' wealth. And she had seen him, too—the impassioned young man behind the impassive face Nick Peters had presented to the world. She had known then he would change her life.

He had, so much so that, when he'd died, she had not been able to go back to that old life. She had tried for a few weeks after the funeral, but eventually she'd returned to her married home in Richmond and her job. It had upset her parents, who'd thought she should make a clean break from both. They had not understood she needed the work to keep herself sane, and she wanted the memories she could only find in the shabby Victorian terrace.

Three years on, her parents still thought the same way and, as time went by, they worried more rather than less about their widowed daughter.

It was one of the reasons Sara limited her visits. She enjoyed being home, especially when her brother's young children were there, but no matter how much she chatted and laughed her parents watched her with anxious eyes. It made her feel rather like a cloud on their otherwise perfect horizon.

This Christmas was no different. She stayed until Boxing Day as arranged, carefully avoided any well-meaning discussions on her private life, then gratefully escaped back to town with her brother Simon. He had offered to drive her home so that he could, as he put it, get away from two screaming kids and as a bonus have the pleasure of her company.

His Jaguar was smooth and relaxing—much like her brother Simon—as, tone studiously casual, he slipped into the conversation, 'So what did you think of Paul?'

'Paul?' For a moment Sara was genuinely at a loss.

'Paul Cartwright—you met him at dinner on Christmas Eve.'

'Oh, *that* Paul.'

'Well?' her brother prompted when no other comment was forthcoming.

'A marginal improvement,' she said succinctly.

It drew a puzzled frown. 'On what?'

'The last one—and don't give me that innocent look,' Sara added, smiling slightly. 'You know as well as I do that mother always finds a spare man for me. Usually on the right side of forty, at least mildly rich, and never, of course, married. Amazing really how she manages it. You wouldn't think there were that many eligible men floating about, would you?'

'All right, sister dear, point taken.' Simon laughed despite himself. 'But may I say you're getting terribly cynical in your old age.'

'Oh, terribly,' she agreed with good humour.

'*And,*' he continued, 'you're actually quite wrong about Paul. For a start, *I* invited him, not Mother. Without any matchmaking intentions, either, I might add. It's just that he's recently taken up a post at the hospital and doesn't know many people in the area.'

'In that case I apologise,' Sara said, not wholly convinced.

Being that much older, Simon had always been protective towards her. As a child, she hadn't minded. However, on occasions he still acted the part of big brother, sure he knew best. She sometimes wondered that, having introduced them, he regarded Nick as his choice. She could only hope he had no ideas of repeating the feat.

He went on, 'Anyway, I understand you're not ready for a serious relationship. I know how special Nick was and how few men could match up to him. He was so brilliant, so able. What he might have done...' Simon trailed off as he shook his head over the things his friend might have achieved if he'd lived.

Sara said nothing. She'd never been able to discuss Nick with anyone, not even Simon. She knew he meant well but she didn't believe he really understood. He had admired Nick for the quickness of his intellect and for his seeming disregard of authority, something a conformist like Simon would never dare to show.

But Sara had loved him for quite different things—for the deep well of compassion behind the tough, competent exterior, for the sudden moments of insecurity that had shown how much he'd needed her. If she'd appreciated his cleverness, it hadn't always been easy to live with, and at times his resistance to authority had seemed just sheer bloody-mindedness. Yes, she'd loved him, but it was for the person he'd been, not the person Simon imagined.

So she said nothing and Simon also lapsed into silence, assuming he'd touched a still raw nerve.

The journey took little time through the sparse traffic. When he turned the car into her street, Sara glanced out of the window and spotted a vaguely familiar figure walking, head bent, in the opposite direction.

'Stop the car!' she cut in so suddenly her brother slammed on the brakes.

'My God, what's wrong?' he demanded, looking about him.

'Nothing drastic. Just someone I think I know,' Sara replied, already half out of the car. 'I'll see you at the house.'

Leaving her surprised brother staring after her, she hurried back up the street until the retreating figure turned at the sound of running footsteps.

'Scott,' she gasped as she caught up with him. 'I thought it was you.'

'Mrs Peters.' The boy smiled in recognition, then said more diffidently, 'I called at your house but you weren't in.'

'No, I've only just arrived back.' Sara sensed his shyness and asked mundanely, 'How did you get here?'

'By bus. I waited for a while but the man upstairs said he didn't know when you were coming home, so I...' he trailed off, obviously uncertain if his visit was welcome.

'Well, it's lucky I didn't miss you,' Sara returned brightly, then not quite truthfully, 'I wondered if you'd call.'

In fact, though the boy had come into her thoughts at odd times in the week, she hadn't expected to see him again. She'd assumed he'd be too busy enjoying what attention he managed to claim from his father.

As they walked back to her house, however, he seemed more like the withdrawn boy she'd first met, and it was plain something was troubling him.

Simon was waiting on the doorstep with her suitcase. Normally she would have offered him coffee, but Scott was already shifting nervously under his curious gaze.

'Look, if I'm intruding, Mrs Peters...' the boy said, backing a step towards the gate.

'Not at all,' Sara assured, and almost laughed at her brother's expression—brows raising at the boy's mannerliness.

She unlocked the front door and led the way inside. Fortunately Simon was sensitive enough to realise his presence was inhibiting her other visitor, and, after depositing her case in the bedroom, he allowed her to hustle him out of the flat.

'Who's he?' He nodded towards the living-room where they'd left Scott. 'Doesn't sound like one of your usual little thugs.'

'*They* are not little thugs and *he* is just a friend,' she replied shortly. 'But thanks for the lift, Simon.'

'OK, OK. I know when I'm not wanted.' He laughed without offence, then suddenly switched to asking, 'Oh, by the way, *did* you like Paul Cartwright?'

'He was all right,' Sara replied, taken by surprise. 'Why?'

'No special reason,' he dismissed casually. 'See you soon—New Year's Eve, if you change your mind about the party.'

He gave her a quick kiss on the cheek before departing with a suspiciously satisfied smile. Sara almost called him back to tell him 'all right' did not mean she wanted to be paired off with the man on her next visit. For all his claims otherwise, she really was beginning to wonder if Simon saw his doctor friend as another suitable choice for her. If that was the case, then big brother was in for a big disappointment.

'Is that your husband?' Scott asked on her return.

'No, my brother Simon,' she told him, and used the opening to explain, 'Actually, I'm a widow.'

'Oh, I didn't realise. I thought you were still quite——' Scott broke off, catching his own tactlessness, but Sara was amused by the half-finished remark, guileless as it was.

'I hope you *were* going to say still quite young, because it's just the sort of boost my ego needs.'

'Yes ... Yes, I was,' the boy confessed with a small smile.

'Good.' She smiled back. 'Now, why don't I make us something to eat? Unless you've had lunch?'

He shook his head and his expression became uneasy once more. Something was definitely wrong, but Sara decided to wait until he was ready to tell her what. She left him looking through her record collection, and went along the outer hall to the back kitchen.

Her fridge was rather bare so she could only make them a quick snack of bacon and egg, but Scott wolfed it down as though he hadn't eaten in days. He caught her quizzical look and mumbled something about missing breakfast. Then, with some gentle prompting, the whole story came spilling out.

Apparently Neville Dryden's mother had arrived two days before Christmas, and, discovering Scott there, had instantly gone into a screeching fit. Eventually Neville had calmed her down and Scott had kept out of her way as much as possible. Somehow they had survived through Christmas, with Neville acting as referee, but that morning they had finally had a head-on collision.

'All I was trying to do was get Neville out of bed so he'd come skating with me. I mean, it was way past eight. How was I to know *she* was still sleeping?' Scott continued in an aggrieved tone. 'And, anyway, *I* didn't start the pillow fight.'

'Pillow fight?' Sara echoed in disbelief. 'You had a pillow fight with her?'

'No, don't be silly!' Scott's slightly scornful look said how ridiculous the idea was. 'With Neville, of course.'

'Oh.' To Sara, the vision of a suave, supercilious Neville Dryden indulging in such horseplay was almost as unlikely.

'He threw a pillow at me when he discovered the time, and that started it,' Scott explained with a fleeting smile. 'We were only fooling about. Not really making that much noise or anything. But I accidentally knocked over a bedside lamp and it must have woken her...'

'What happened then?' Sara guessed it wasn't going to be pleasant.

'She came storming in and half tripped over my sports-bag.' He indicated the holdall he'd brought with him. 'So she began yelling things at me. Neville told her to shut up but she wouldn't. I tried to ignore her like he says to, but when she started calling my mother names, I sort of lost my temper.'

'What did you do, Scott?' she pressed gently.

'I—um—I told her she was a *stupid old cow*,' he confessed in a rush, then appealed of Sara, 'I suppose that's pretty awful?'

'I've heard worse,' she responded, his rudeness mild compared to what some kids might have said. 'How did his mother react?'

'Well, she stopped screaming at least.' Scott pulled a face. 'But if looks could kill, boy, would I have been dead!'

'And Neville?' Sara prompted.

Scott bit his lip. It was obviously Dryden's reaction which really concerned him. 'I'm not sure. His mother took a step towards me, and I just ran. But I heard him shouting after me and he sounded mad.'

'This was about eight o'clock?' Sara checked her watch—more than five hours ago.

'Yes, I walked around for a couple of hours before I came here,' he accounted for the missing hours, although that was not Sara's main worry. Much as she disliked the man, she felt Dryden should be informed where the boy was.

'I thought about going skating,' Scott ran on, 'but it's not much fun on your own. Besides, I can't yet. I only got the boots for Christmas.'

'From Neville?' Her guess was confirmed by an enthusiastic nod.

'Would you like to see them?' he offered, already digging into his bag.

Sara examined the skate she was handed, and was genuinely impressed. 'Leinmann. That's a very good make.'

Scott's face brightened. 'Can you skate?'

'I used to be able to in my teens,' Sara admitted, 'but I was never competitive class or anything.'

'You liked it though?' he pursued, and she caught on.

'Yes, but listen, Scott, I think you should phone home before we decide on anything else,' she said firmly. 'You've been gone quite a while and Neville was probably expecting you back by lunch. He may be worrying about what's happened to you.'

The boy frowned. 'I suppose I've made things worse. What do you think?'

'I don't know, Scott,' she sighed, 'but I'll have to telephone him if you won't.'

'Maybe that would be better,' he suggested hopefully.

From past experience, Sara doubted it. But she gave way to the pleading blue eyes turned on her, and consoled herself that at least this time she was forewarned about Neville Dryden.

She called from the phone in the hallway. A voice answered almost immediately, repeating the number, and Sara's heart raced a little as she recognised the resonant, drawling tones.

She took a deep, calming breath, before saying, 'Mr Dryden?'

'Speaking,' he confirmed.

'I—it's Mrs Peters,' Sara went on, feeling ridiculously nervous. 'We met——'

'At Fulham Police Station,' he supplied for her. 'Yes, I remember.'

Sara was amazed that he did, and felt an odd sense of satisfaction. Then she shook her head at her silliness and told herself to get on with it.

'It's about Scott——' she resumed, only to be interrupted again.

'Scott? Have you seen him?' he asked, not hiding his anxiety.

'Yes, he's here with me now,' Sara told him quickly, and waited for his tone to change to annoyance.

Instead there was an audible sigh of relief, followed by a heartfelt, 'Thank God!' from the other end, before he continued, 'He had a three-rounder with my mother this morning and ran off. But I suppose he's told you all this?'

'Well, yes,' Sara returned carefully, 'he did say he'd disturbed your mother's sleep and an argument ensued.'

'That's one way of putting it.' Neville Dryden laughed at her sanitised account. 'You should have heard what the brat called her.'

'I did,' Sara admitted, then thought it wise to add, 'He's asked me to apologise on his behalf. He didn't mean to be quite so rude.'

'Oh, well, tell him he's forgiven,' Neville said easily, making it clear whose side he was on. 'Between you and me, his choice of words may not have been too polite, but it was singularly accurate. As silly cows go, my mother is definitely in the Oscar-winning category,' he stated with grim amusement.

It led Sara to ask, 'Is she likely to forgive Scott?'

'When hell freezes over, possibly,' Neville confided drily, 'but don't worry. I've just her offered an all-expenses paid vacation in Antigua in return for her early departure. She's upstairs at the moment, either packing or sulking, I'm not sure which, but with any luck she'll be airborne by late afternoon.'

'I see. What about Scott in the meantime? Should I bring him home?' Sara wanted any suggestions to come from him. She did not altogether trust this new, more approachable Neville Dryden and she had no wish to be accused of interference.

'I'd be grateful if you could.' His tone remained warm and friendly. 'Or perhaps it would be better if I came and collected him? I can't right now, but after my mother's gone I could drive round.'

'It's all right.' Sara felt an odd panic at the idea of meeting him again, even briefly, and decided it was a thing to be avoided. 'I thought I might take Scott skating up at the Queensway rink. It's the nearest to you in Chelsea and, from there, I can deliver him home by taxi.'

'Well, I know the squirt would like that,' he responded, 'but are you sure? You are on holiday, and Mr Peters can't be over-enamoured spending it playing nursemaid.'

'Mr Peters?' she repeated dumbly.

'Your husband,' he reminded on a wry note.

'Oh.' Caught on the hop, Sara decided against announcing her widowhood. It seemed an unnecessary complication. 'No, it's fine,' she said instead. 'Scott's no trouble.'

'Well, that's debatable,' Neville said. 'However, I won't dissuade you. It's a relief to know he's with someone...responsible.'

And dull, and ordinary, Sara imagined him mentally adding, as any compliment was lost on her.

When he ran on, 'Anyway, I really can't thank you enough——' she cut him short.

'It's nothing. I'll see he gets home, Mr Dryden,' she said rather primly, then rang off. She might be dull and ordinary but she wasn't desperate. He could waste his charm on someone else.

She stood in the hallway for a moment, collecting herself and wondering why Neville Dryden had such an

effect on her. Though he hadn't been arrogant or supercilious this time, she'd still reacted adversely. Throughout
the conversation she'd been aware of him as a man pow-
erfully attractive to other women and confident of the
fact, and it made her determined not to be susceptible.
If she came over as prickly and defensive, that was too
bad.

'Was he very mad?' Scott asked when she slipped back
into the flat.

Sara reassured him, 'No, not at all. He was just glad
to know where you were.'

'Oh, good. I should have realised Neville would be
OK,' the boy said with hindsight. 'He's always pretty
fair, even though she's his mother. Did he say anything
about what I called her?'

Sara hesitated, then shook her head, deciding not to
pass on Neville Dryden's 'singularly accurate' comment.
Scott didn't need any encouragement to be precocious.

'But it's all right if I go skating with you?' Scott appealed, now his anxiety had disappeared.

'Yes . . . Yes, it is.' Sara pushed aside any reservations
she had and smiled back. Taking the boy to the ice rink
was hardly becoming over-involved, and Neville Dryden
had *asked* for her help.

It was not how she'd planned to spend the afternoon,
of course, but she didn't grudge the time as they travelled by bus to the Queensway ice rink. Where it took
a real effort to like some of the children her brother
termed 'little thugs', Scott was a different matter. Quick,
amusing and talkative, he made her smile even when she
felt she shouldn't. It was hard not to, because, for all
the worldly cynicism he affected, there was an under-
lying eagerness that cancelled it out.

By the time they reached the ice rink Sara was
thoroughly enjoying herself. She'd forgotten what fun
skating was, and, after some initial coaxing to leave the
safety of the barrier, Scott proved a good pupil. If, at

first, he spent more time sitting on the ice than skating over it, he took his falls with a grin. And, when he eventually found his balance, he progressed rapidly until he no longer needed her hand for confidence.

Eventually Sara retired to the side for a rest. She couldn't match his energy but she was quite happy to watch him, giving the occasional wave of encouragement as he passed. She would wait until he tired, then deliver him to Dryden's doorstep, hopefully avoiding any encounter with the man himself.

At least, that was her plan before Scott suddenly skated towards her, almost crashing into the barrier in his excitement.

'Why didn't you tell me Neville was coming?' he asked, grinning from ear to ear.

Sara prayed she'd misheard the question. 'Sorry?'

'Neville—he's over there. Isn't that great?'

Great, Sara thought; why in heaven's name had he turned up?

She scanned the far side of the rink, saying, 'I can't see him.'

'There he is!' Scott pointed towards the entrance but Sara was still unable to spot the man. She was just beginning to wonder how reliable her new contact lenses were, when Scott added helpfully, 'He's wearing a leather jacket and jeans.'

Sara had already passed over the tall figure in dark brown battle-jacket and cream cords. He bore little resemblance to the Neville Dryden of a week ago, and she blinked. 'Not the man with the beard and dark glasses?'

'Yes, that's Neville.' Scott laughed at her incredulous expression. 'Come on, he hasn't noticed us yet.'

Following with reluctance, Sara wasn't convinced she had the right man until they crossed the rink and he began walking towards the barrier. Then there was something all too familiar about the smile flashed at them from behind a shadowy growth of beard and dark-lensed glasses. And somehow, despite his almost scruffy appearance, he still managed to look striking.

For just a second Sara felt it—the compelling attraction of the man—and her heart gave a peculiar twist. But sanity prevailed as his smile widened and she told herself not to be such a damn idiot.

'Did you see me, Neville?' demanded Scott as he slid to a rather inelegant halt.

'Pretty good, squirt. I didn't realise you'd been skating before,' Dryden said, so straight-faced that only Sara realised he was teasing.

Scott beamed at the hidden compliment before protesting, 'I haven't—ask Sara!'

'Sara?' The man lifted a brow at the familiarity.

'Mrs Peters. She said it was OK if I used her first name. Didn't you?' Scott's appeal drew a nod of approval from Sara. '*And* she taught me how to skate,' he added.

'Did she, now?' Dryden's attention switched to Sara, eyes unreadable behind the dark glasses but lingering too long to be simple politeness.

She also looked very different from the first time they'd met. Her hair was no longer caught in a severe bun, but fell in loose, natural waves, framing her high cheekbones and wide dark eyes. And, though her jeans and sweater could hardly be termed fashionable, they revealed long, shapely legs and firm, well-rounded breasts, emphasised by her slimness. Hers was a figure most men would have considered worth a second glance.

Neville Dryden was no exception. Several seconds passed before he broke off his silent appraisal to add, 'That was good of her.'

By that time Sara's face was suffused with angry colour, viewing his admiring stare as merely rude and his comment insincere. She positively scowled when he favoured her with another of his lazy smiles.

The smile faded rapidly.

Puzzled, Scott looked from one to the other, aware Neville had somehow upset Sara and, from his darkening expression, was about to upset her even more. Unless, of course, someone created a distraction.

'Listen, Neville,' he plunged in bravely, 'I'm sorry about this morning. I suppose I shouldn't have called your mother names.'

Dryden's gaze remained on Sara some seconds longer before, visibly shrugging off anger, he turned to the boy.

'No, probably not,' he agreed in his languid drawl, 'but, in the light of subsequent events, I forgive you.'

'Subsequent events?' Scott echoed.

'Dear Felice decided to depart for sunnier climes,' Dryden relayed.

'Honestly?' Scott was plainly delighted.

Sara was more confused, wondering who the 'dear Felice' could be. How many women did Neville Dryden have in his life, for goodness' sake?

Her disapproving frown was observed, and in a very wry tone she was informed, 'Felice is my *mother's* name, Mrs Peters.'

'I realised that, Mr Dryden,' she lied coolly, determined not to be disconcerted.

'Of course.' He gave her a sceptically amused look.

Sara decided it was time to depart herself. 'Well, I'd better be running along,' she said with a smile solely for Scott's benefit.

'But Neville's just got here,' the boy protested innocently.

'Quite,' the man put in drily, knowing full well that was the exact reason Sara intended leaving.

Bright though Scott was, the undercurrents passed him by. He simply thought Neville was agreeing that Sara should stay.

'So you can't go yet,' he concluded and gave her a lop-sided grin she didn't have the heart to argue against. 'Neville's going to skate with us, aren't you?'

The actor glanced doubtfully at the rink. 'I don't know, squirt. It's pretty crowded.'

'Oh, go on, Neville!' Scott urged. 'It's not as bad as it looks. Is it, Sara?'

'No... at least, not if one *can* skate,' Sara couldn't resist murmuring.

Picking up the soft mockery in her voice, Dryden countered, 'And if one can't?'

But, before Sara could find a suitable reply, he ran on, 'Still, I suppose you're right and it's very kind of you to offer, Mrs Peters... or may I call you Sara?'

'Offer?' Sara echoed, confused by the sudden shift in conversation and missing his broad wink at Scott.

'A skating lesson, of course. Unless I'm being presumptuous?'

That was one word for it, Sara fumed, but she could hardly voice any of the others that came to mind. Not in front of Scott, at any rate. She limited herself to pointing out, 'You haven't any skates.'

'True, but I'm sure I can hire some,' he drawled back, and went to do just that with a murmur of, 'Don't go away, will you?'

Outmanoeuvred, Sara stared at his retreating back. She couldn't decide whether to be angry or just plain exasperated, and she glanced towards Scott.

He too seemed uncertain. While his eyes slid away from hers, his mouth had a distinctly amused curve, and, mumbling an excuse of needing more practice, he, too, deserted her.

Sara was left alone, wondering how she'd landed herself in such a situation and how she might possibly get out of it.

CHAPTER FOUR

'OK, I'M ready.' Dryden reappeared at her side in record time, to lean against the barrier, arms folded, boots on, awaiting instructions.

Not knowing where to start, Sara stood there, avoiding the gaze of blue eyes no longer concealed by dark glasses. Teaching Scott was one thing, Neville Dryden quite another. She wasn't about to lead *him* by the hand.

'It's sort of like riding a bike,' she finally volunteered. 'You just have to get on and find your balance, really.'

'Sounds easy,' Dryden returned, irritatingly confident.

'It's not *that* easy!' Sara was snapping back before she could stop herself, supporting the idea that he *did* need her help.

'No, I'm sure it's not,' he agreed quickly, an appeasing note in his voice.

Being humoured irritated Sara even more. She was tempted to skate off and leave him to it, but was forestalled from such a move.

'Well, let's go, before I lose my nerve,' he said, smile flashing, and, with more than enough nerve for Sara's liking, grasped her hand in his, adding, 'Don't worry. If I feel in danger of falling, I won't take you with me.'

Without noticing *he* had actually led the way on to the ice, Sara realised it would be silly to over-react to the simple touch of his hand. So she fell silent and let him use her for balance.

They circled the rink once and he managed to remain on his feet throughout. Admittedly he had allowed her to lead him round at a snail's pace, his movements cautious and stiff. Yet, apart from the occasional wobble, he kept his balance remarkably well.

'Do you know, I think I'm getting the hang of it,' he said, as they began a second lap.

'I wouldn't get too confident,' she muttered back, practically the only advice she'd given.

A natural teacher where Scott was concerned, Sara was too self-conscious with Dryden, too aware of the hard, warm grip of the hand holding hers. It was absurd to be so sensitive. To hold her breath when his fingers closed tighter over hers. It didn't seem to matter that his amused look said he was playing with her—as he'd played with so many women, in his effortlessly charming, utterly meaningless way.

With all her efforts concentrated on resisting him, perhaps Sara's lack of perception was excusable. And it did happen very gradually—so gradually she didn't even notice the change at first. Didn't realise she was no longer deciding the pace before she suddenly found herself speeding to keep up. Didn't fully understand until the moment he executed a neat turn to face her. Then she understood too well. For no one—but no one—skated backwards after a ten-minute lesson!

'You—you can skate!' she spluttered, only to have her words deliberately misinterpreted.

'Good heavens, so I can!' he said as though it were a revelation to him, too, and, eyes positively alive with laughter, claimed, 'I guess I'm a quick learner.'

If she'd had the chance, Sara might possibly have struck him, but he suddenly took off again, her hand clasped firmly clasped in his own, and, after that, it required all her skill to follow him.

'Done any pairs skating?' he threw at her and she, like an idiot, nodded.

The next moment he drew her into the circle of his arms, held her close for a second or two, then, laughing at her alarmed expression, launched them into a dance sequence to the beat of the overhead music. It was very much an up-tempo number, and Sara could only follow as he weaved a path through the crowd. He carried her with him, through each twist and turn, using his strength to match her body's line to his and making her feel as light as a dancer. She did little else but hold on and go with the flow.

By the time he skated them back to the side, she was no longer gasping with outrage, she was just gasping! She didn't even object to the arm still lightly encircling her waist. She wasn't sure that if he took it away she wouldn't fall down.

He, on the other hand, showed very little sign of breathlessness as he remarked, 'Hey, you're quite good . . . for an amateur.'

At that Sara slipped his hold and countered smartly, 'You're not bad yourself, Mr Dryden . . . *for a beginner*.'

He laughed out loud and for once his laugh had a pleasant sound, genuinely amused rather than sarcastic. Sara pulled a face in response, admitting the joke had been on her. Then Scott reappeared, having watched from the sidelines.

'Wow, you were really good!' he said, eyes full of admiration for the way she'd kept up with Neville. 'I bet you knew all the time he could skate.'

Just wishing she'd been that smart, Sara returned his grin with a wink.

'What about me, squirt—or didn't I rate any notice?' Neville said drily.

'You were OK, I suppose,' Scott replied, the faint praise deliberate as he added for Sara's benefit, 'He should be. He was coached by a world champion once, for a film part.'

'Thank you, squirt.' Neville's expression was wry as Scott blackened his case further.

Uninhibited, the boy went on to confide, '*And* he broke his ankle the first day.'

'Did he, now?' Sara turned amused eyes in Neville's direction.

'Rubbish!' he dismissed, before correcting, 'It was the second day, not the first, *and* it was only a sprain.'

The two males laughed together, and Sara found herself joining in. If she didn't like the man very much, he did have a sense of humour and, as she was beginning to realise, an undoubted fondness for Scott.

It was plain when the boy begged for more time on the ice, and Neville gave way easily, 'All right, pest. Half an hour. We'll be in the café over there.'

Of course his arrogance was less appealing as he took for granted that Sara would share a coffee with him. Still, he was polite about it, as he organised their change in footwear, then installed her in a seat before queuing at the café counter.

Sara just wished she knew why he was bothering.

'Do you smoke? I can't remember,' he said in the silence that had fallen when he returned with the coffee.

'I'm trying to give up——' Sara hesitated, then, noticing the packet offered was not the decadent-looking Russian brand, succumbed to temptation. 'Not very successfully, I'm afraid.'

He made a sympathetic face as he flicked a lighter to her cigarette. 'I'm having the same problem myself, despite Scott's efforts on my behalf.'

'Scott's efforts?'

'Every time I light up, he gives me a look that would make a pious nun feel guilty. Unfortunately, it hasn't been too effective in my case.' A low laugh suggested his conscience was not so easily stirred. 'He's a good kid though.'

'Yes.' Sara smiled in agreement.

'A bit mixed-up, perhaps,' he continued, 'but not as much as he may appear.'

This time Sara frowned, wondering where the conversation was leading. That it was leading somewhere she gathered from the suddenly serious gaze trained on her. Did he think her interest in Scott professional?

'Actually I find him a very likeable boy,' she replied, and was content to leave it at that.

Dryden wasn't. 'Yes, well, I'm grateful to you for looking after him this afternoon. I only hope you won't read too much into the earlier incident ... or feel obliged to pursue the matter.'

Obviously choosing his words with care, he still succeeded in getting Sara's back up. It might be phrased more politely, but the message was the same as the one he'd sent the first night at the police station: stay out of my business!

That she had no intention of involving herself in it did not stop Sara from saying, 'I'm not sure what you mean, Mr Dryden. I understood from Scott that he disturbed your mother's sleep and it led to a quarrel. What else *could* I read into that?'

Dryden did not reply immediately. From the look he gave her, he was having difficulty deciding if she was being deliberately awkward or merely obtuse.

'I think you might have misunderstood me, Mrs Peters,' he eventually said. 'If I may be frank ... ?'

'By all means, Mr Dryden,' she invited coolly, and received an irritable frown.

It was matched by his tone as he went on, 'I wish to be sure you realise there is no need to concern yourself over Scott's welfare. He may seem what you'd term a problem child, but—whether he is or not—I'm certain it would not be in his interests to be treated as one.'

'Or your interests either, Mr Dryden, perhaps?' Sara suggested with a hint of contempt.

'Mine?' His face darkened to a scowl. 'I have nothing to hide if that's what you're implying. I just don't wish Scott to be made more of an exception than he already is. And, however well-meaning you believe your intentions, you won't do him any favours by interfering.'

In some respects, Sara did not discount what Dryden was saying. There were children whose situations, if far from perfect, were better left alone; she'd already decided that Scott's was one. But, being warned off—especially in this fashion—was hardly an appeal to reason.

'I trust I've made myself clear,' he added after several seconds had passed and her only reply was a stare as hard as his own.

'As crystal, Mr Dryden,' she said shortly.

'Well?' he prompted.

'May I also be frank?'

'I'd appreciate it.'

From the edge in his voice, Sara doubted it, but she continued, regardless. 'In that case, Mr Dryden, you're right—I do think Scott has problems.' She levelled him a look that put him at the top of the list. 'However, much as I like him, I have absolutely no desire to tackle them. For one thing, I don't need to tout for business. I have quite enough victims on whom to practise—what was the phrase—my well-meaning intentions, yes? And, for another, as callous as it may sound, the problems of a poor little rich kid like Scott don't even touch on the scale suffered by the children I normally deal with.'

Point made, Sara watched his expression undergo a series of changes ranging from anger to disbelief. Not only had Neville Dryden overrated her interest in his business, he had vastly underrated her ability to hold her own.

'I trust I've also made myself clear, Mr Dryden,' she finally echoed, in a parody of his earlier words.

'Cuttingly, Mrs Peters,' he confirmed, and Sara decided to quit while she was ahead.

'So if you'll excuse me,' she said, thinking he'd be satisfied to end the conversation there.

A hand shot out at her move to rise. 'You're not walking away, are you, without giving me a chance at least?'

'To do what?' She frowned at the fingers gripping her wrist.

'To apologise, naturally,' he said with a slight drawl, but dropped it as he conceded, 'Obviously I was quite out of line. I won't say I enjoyed being put straight, but I expect I had it coming.'

It was hardly an abject apology, but, coming from Neville Dryden, Sara suspected it was the closest she'd get.

She was left with the choice of accepting gracefully or struggling to escape his hold. In the end she took a middle course, sinking back in her chair with an expression on the hostile side of suspicious.

'You know, you're very different from how I imagined the other night,' he said after he'd released her hand and taken to staring at her again, this time as if she were an interesting curiosity. 'Less grimly righteous and much more hard-headed. That's a compliment, by the way,' he felt obliged to relay.

'I'm glad you told me,' Sara put in drily.

'Anyway,' he ignored her sarcasm, 'I had this idea you were the reforming type, hence the misguided lecture. I suppose the image threw me.'

'Image?' she queried, although she had a feeling she shouldn't.

'The spinsterish bun and glasses you were wearing,' he volunteered, and had the nerve to smile. 'Very deceptive. Still, I imagine looking dowdy might be an advantage in your line of work.'

Sara couldn't quite make up her mind if he was being deliberately offensive or was managing it without effort. But she mustered as much grim righteousness as she could to reply, 'I don't go in for images, Mr Dryden. I arrange my hair for neatness and I wear glasses because I can see less than a yard without them.'

'Really?' Dryden met the large dark eyes which seemed so sharply focused on him. 'Then I must be a blur to you.'

'*Unfortunately*, no,' Sara retorted. 'I'm wearing contact lenses.'

Maddeningly, the insult drew nothing more than an amused laugh, before he drawled back, 'You know, you should use the lenses all the time. If you don't mind my saying so, Mrs Peters, you have remarkably beautiful eyes.'

Sara decided she *did* mind him saying so. She'd already had enough of her appearance being the topic of conversation, and felt it was time to turn the spotlight back on him. After all, he was used to it.

'You look rather different yourself, Mr Dryden,' she said, eyes flicking from his unshaven face and dark glasses to the fur-collared flying jacket worn over a Shetland sweater. 'Is this some new image you're going in for—downmarket casual?'

He laughed again, unoffended. 'More of a disguise, you might say.'

'Disguise?'

'It guarantees a certain degree of anonymity.'

'Ah, yes, I forgot. You're an actor, aren't you?' she said with subtle disdain. 'Scott tells me you're quite well-known.'

'I thought I was,' he replied on a wry note. 'Scott tells me you've never heard of me.'

'Well, I shouldn't worry too much about it,' she jibed. 'I understand I'm in a minority.'

'Oh, I'm not worried, Mrs Peters.' His careless drawl supported the claim. 'My ego may be as large as you imply but it's hardly as fragile.'

Fifteen all, Sara thought, suddenly aware the conversation was developing into a sparring match and not about to throw in the towel.

'Did *I* imply that, Mr Dryden?' she returned archly.

'You damn well know you did,' he laughed back, then surprised her with his bluntness, 'Tell me—is it just actors in general or me in particular you dislike?'

Altogether too direct, Sara tried to duck the question. 'I don't know any other actors,' she said with a shrug, not realising the way it might be taken.

'So it must be me,' Dryden was quick to conclude. 'I wonder why. I suppose that first telephone conversation was not the most auspicious beginning to a relationship.'

His choice of words made Sara declare with equal bluntness, 'Mr Dryden, as far as I'm concerned, we don't have a relationship, beginning or otherwise. Any interest I have is in Scott and, in case you've forgotten, you've just finished warning me to drop it or else.'

'No, I haven't forgotten.' He paused, and his stare became calculating. 'But maybe I've changed my mind.'

'About what, precisely?'

'You and Scott. He likes you and he doesn't like many people, especially women. Perhaps he does need some counselling. On a strictly unofficial basis, you understand.'

'Mr Dryden——' Sara intended telling him she didn't want to get involved.

'Neville,' he cut in with a smile. 'It's surely not too compromising to be on first-name terms. I have received the message, you know.'

'Message?'

'That you have no personal interest in me...as a man, I mean,' he added, and Sara's blank look became one of unmistakable astonishment. 'Or didn't you realise you were sending it?'

'I think you have your wires crossed, *Mr Dryden*,' she replied heavily. 'I'm not sure if it's your conceit or mine that's in question, but why should I feel the need to advertise such a fact? Apart from anything else, we're not exactly each other's type.'

'Aren't we?' The soft challenge sounded almost serious, but her stony expression made him laugh shortly, 'No, perhaps not. I take it young blabbermouth told you I have a predilection for women without too much, let's say, intellect.'

Rather than admit Scott had done just that, Sara pointed out, 'I did meet your current girlfriend, if you recall.'

'Ah, yes... Janey,' he said as if he really did have difficulty recollecting the name. 'She's not a girlfriend as such. But true, I do normally prefer the dumb blonde type. More wearing on the nerves, possibly, but less of a threat to my status.'

'You mean as a celebrity?' Sara quizzed and was awarded an irritated look.

'One of us seems very hung up on my supposed fame, and it's *not* me.'

'Then what did you mean?'

'Actually, I was referring to my status as a happily *un*-married man.'

'Oh,' Sara sniffed, and there was a wealth of disapproval in the syllable. So that was why poor Scott was illegitimate.

'Not that I'm against marriage in principle, you understand,' Dryden went on, adding fuel to the fire. 'In fact, I've heard rumours it works for some people.'

'Must you be so cynical?' Sara snapped angrily. 'Have you any idea what sort of influence you are having on Scott?'

'Obviously not a good one in your opinion,' he replied, sounding unconcerned by the fact. 'But, believe it or not, I do have some scruples. For one, he's away at school much of the time. And, when he's home, I always do my—er—entertaining elsewhere. I even have a certain respect for marriage.'

'It doesn't show,' she told him.

'Doesn't it?' A mocking brow was raised. 'And there was I, resisting the temptation to tell you what an absolutely stunning body you have and how attracted I am to it. I'm not shocking you, am I?' he asked as a small gasp escaped Sara's lips.

'No,' she ground out, not ready to admit it.

'Good, because I was merely illustrating what I mean by respect,' he drawled on. 'You see, if you weren't a married lady, I might be tempted to do something about that attraction, but as it is...' He gave an expressive shrug.

Only the feeling that he might be trying to provoke her stopped Sara from exploding. She was damned if she was going to give him the satisfaction.

'You can't imagine what a relief that is, Mr Dryden,' she eventually said through gritted teeth.

'*Neville,*' he corrected again, bland in the face of her sarcasm. 'So what's he like, your other half?'

'What?' The sudden question threw her totally.

'Your husband,' he added, assuming she hadn't understood.

'Why do you want to know?' Sara demanded suspiciously as she recovered her balance.

'No special reason.' He shrugged. 'I just thought I'd better move the conversation to a safer topic before Scott appears.'

'I see,' she muttered back.

'You could start with what he does for a living,' he prompted, regardless of her obvious reluctance to say more. 'Something worthy, I'll be bound.'

'He's...he's a doctor,' Sara found herself replying.

'Very worthy,' Dryden commented with a thin smile. 'GP or hospital?'

'Hospital.' Again she avoided the truth and, in blushing, stirred his curiosity.

'Which one?' he pursued.

'The——' Sara hesitated, then decided it was absurd not to state she was widowed. 'Look, if you must know,' she changed to saying, but he no longer seemed to be listening.

She watched him raise a hand in signal, and turned to see Scott bearing down on them. On the whole, she was relieved at the distraction.

That was before she discovered the man wasn't so easily side-tracked, coming right back to the subject when Scott was seated.

'I was just asking Mrs Peters about her husband,' he remarked casually enough, but his enquiring gaze rested on Sara.

She felt more uncomfortable than ever. She must have looked it, too, as a well-intentioned Scott leapt to her rescue. Unfortunately his method was a little crude.

It drew a pained wince from Dryden, before he switched his eyes to the boy, saying, 'There appears to be a horse under the table.'

Scott made no reply but coloured slightly at this reference to his over-enthusiastic kick.

'Or are you trying to tell me something?' the man continued in a drawl. 'If so, words will suffice.'

What a sarcastic brute he really was! Sara fumed, as the boy squirmed in embarrassment.

'Mr Dryden,' she cut in, forgetting her own discomfort, 'I think Scott was trying to be tactful. You see, he knows I'm a widow.'

It drew a surprised look that predictably changed to mockery. 'Does he indeed? Well, it seems he was to be privileged with more information than I.'

'I *was* about to tell you!' she insisted.

'Were you? Somehow I doubt that.' His lips gave a cynical twist. 'You wouldn't, by any chance, have taken what I was saying earlier seriously, would you?'

'No, of course not!' she snapped back.

'You should have, you know.' It sounded almost like a threat, before he bluntly asked, 'You're not a recent widow, are you?'

It was at this point Scott hissed, 'Neville, stop it!' and received a frown for interrupting.

'Stop what, precisely?' Dryden demanded.

'*You* know!' accused Scott.

Worriedly, Sara watched them eyeing each other across the table. Once again she was struck by their likeness, from the straight, handsome features to the dramatic blue-eyed, black-haired colouring. She felt responsible for the sullen defiance now on the boy's face and the grim warning on the man's.

'It's OK, Scott.' She touched his arm. 'I'm not upset.'

But Scott was determined to side with her, muttering, 'He has no reason to be like that to you.'

The criticism did not go down well—not well at all. Sara watched as the man's jaw clenched with contained anger.

'All right, Scott, that's enough,' he clipped back. 'I doubt Mrs Peters needs you to champion her, but I'm not going to debate the point. So I suggest we just go, mm?'

He rose to his feet, making it plain he did not expect any argument. Although Scott's mouth was still set in a stubborn line, he had the sense to say no more on the subject. Instead, with a show of reluctance, he followed.

Naturally Sara assumed she was not included in Dryden's all but spoken order. Yet, when she remained seated, she too was awarded an imperative stare.

'Mrs Peters, I shall, of course, drive you home.'

'That's not necessary. I can get a bus.'

'I insist.'

Polite banalities, they were said with an undercurrent of anything but politeness. Sara realised she was in for a rerun of the bus-stop scene, minus the rain. This time she was quite sure she could have outlasted him. If only she'd been immune to the appeal in Scott's eyes, that was.

When they emerged from the ice rink, Dryden left them in the doorway while he fetched his car, parked some streets away. By the time he picked them up, he had returned to being charming—too much so for Sara's liking. But she felt no suspicion when he drove to his Chelsea home, ostensibly to drop Scott off first.

Perhaps it really wasn't part of a prearranged plan, for his manner was quite casual as he pulled up outside an elegant Georgian town house and said, 'Look, it's past six. You may as well come in and have dinner with us.'

It was hardly the most gracious invitation Sara had ever had, and certainly not a welcome one. But, before she could refuse, he was out of the car and coming round to open her door. With little alternative, she climbed out while he dispatched Scott to inform someone called James that there would, once again, be three for dinner.

Only then did he notice her mutinous expression and had the effrontery to ask, 'What's wrong now?'

'I don't suppose it's occurred to you that *I* might already have plans for this evening,' she replied heavily.

'No,' he admitted without apology. 'Why? Have you?'

'That's not the point!' she snapped in reply.

It had no visible effect, however, as he smiled and said, 'I take it that means you haven't,' and, ignoring her glare, curled his fingers round an elbow to almost push her up the front steps.

In exasperation, she turned on him. 'You are, without doubt, the most arrogant, egotistical——'

'Yes, I know,' he interrupted, laughing, and, with the appearance of a poker-faced butler in the doorway, effectively had the last word.

This time, at least, thought Sara, determined there wouldn't be a next.

CHAPTER FIVE

NOT unfamiliar with the trappings of wealth, Sara was still impressed by the size of Neville's Georgian house. The entrance hall alone, with its chequered marble floor and wide staircase, could have swallowed much of her Richmond home. Leading off it, the reception-rooms were in the same grand style, high-ceilinged, dominated by great old-fashioned fireplaces and furnished in antique walnut and leather. Yet the overall effect was one of understated elegance, not in the least what she'd expected from the actor.

There was a single feature which she considered out and out ostentation. It was a portrait above the living-room fireplace. Done in oils, its traditional style suited the surroundings, but any artistic merit she dismissed after a bare glance at the face of the sitter.

Her disdain must have shown, as Dryden asked if it was the subject or the painting which was not to her taste. She didn't quite match his frankness but made enough oblique remarks to imply that hanging one's own portrait in one's own living-room was the act of an ego-maniac.

In doing so, she also managed to make a complete fool of herself. For, at his wry suggestion she examine the portrait more closely, she gave it another contemptuous stare, only to realise the sitter wasn't Neville Dryden. The colouring and the haughty, handsome features were the same, or at least sufficiently similar to be deceptive at first glance, but they did not belong to the man standing beside her, looking amused as the devil.

He sounded it, too, as he explained that the gentleman, in what she now recognised to be a pre-War morning suit, was Henry Dryden, late owner of the Chelsea house and grandfather to its present occupant.

He went on to give her a brief account of Dryden family history. Apparently the last four generations had been connected with the theatre in some form or other. It had started with a great-grandmother, a star of Victorian music halls before she had 'gone respectable' to marry a man of property. Their son, Henry of the portrait, although following his father into business, had invested much of the family money in various theatrical ventures, including a rather extravagant actress wife.

Fortune, however, had not smiled on Henry. The ventures had flourished but the marriage had not. Eventually the actress wife had decamped with a dubious Italian count, leaving their young son behind.

The son David, Neville's own father, had taken after his mother and, under an assumed name, had turned to a career on the stage. In the post-war period he had been lured to Hollywood, where British actors had been all the rage.

It was at this point in the narrative that Sara exclaimed, 'David Hanson—why, I've heard of him!' Then, realising her tactlessness, she made it worse by adding, 'I mean, he was very famous, wasn't he? Not that you're not or anything. You probably are. It's just that . . . I think I'd better shut up,' she eventually trailed off.

Neville, however, seemed amused by her stammerings, unconcerned that his father had made an impression where he hadn't. Later Sara was to read in a magazine that, if Dryden senior had been a big star of the American cinema, his son was actually regarded as the better actor.

'You may have heard of my mother too—Felice Devereux,' he added drily.

'The name is familiar,' Sara admitted, 'but I can't picture the face.'

'Apart from a few early pictures with my father, she was never very successful.' He shrugged. 'Between her accented English and her uncertain temperament, she was considered a director's nightmare.'

The criticism was said in a humorous vein but without any trace of indulgence. It made Sara wonder if the temperamental Felice had also been something of a nightmare as a mother.

'Were you brought up in America?' she asked out of curiosity.

'Until I was six,' he confirmed. 'Then my grandfather arrived on the scene, decided I needed saving from the combined fate of Felice and Hollywood, and took me back with him to be educated in England.'

This time there was a certain fondness in his reference to Henry of the portrait, suggesting he hadn't objected to being saved. Presumably his parents, busy with their careers, hadn't minded the arrangement either, but Sara couldn't help thinking his own careless childhood might, in part, be responsible for his casual approach to Scott's. Perhaps he just didn't know any better.

Certainly, after sitting through a dinner with the two, she could no longer believe he was in any way indifferent to the boy. He might avoid acknowledging his parentage, often addressing him with that offhand 'squirt', never an affectionate 'son', but there was an affinity between the two, stronger than in many conventional relationships.

They laughed at the same things, they finished each other's sentences, and, in place of Dryden's earlier sarcasm, there was an almost gentle irony. He talked to Scott as though he enjoyed his company, and occasionally Sara glimpsed, under the blasé front, a pride in the boy's quick intelligence. As for Scott, if he had proved aware of the man's faults, he obviously forgave them all.

During the early stages of the meal, Sara took little part in the conversation. With Scott present, she was prepared to be civil to Dryden, but that was all. Yet, as the evening wore on, she found herself relaxing her guard and laughing aloud at some of his humorous anecdotes about the film world. It was Scott who encouraged these stories and, several times, she caught the boy smiling at her, as if to say, 'See, I told you Neville was fun.'

It was natural enough, she supposed, that he wanted her to share his admiration of the man, but she could have warned him not to rely on it. Amusing Neville might be. Admirable, she doubted.

After dinner they returned to the lounge for coffee, served by the formidable James. He was still in starched butler attire, still as poker-faced as ever—the model of a dignified manservant.

So it was something of a shock to hear Scott say, 'Fancy some gin later, Jim?'

And more of one when the manservant, without batting an eyelid, replied, 'Certainly, Master Scott, I'll be in the kitchen,' before withdrawing with a formal bow.

Sara was left open-mouthed at the exchange, and, for once, Neville took pity on her, explaining that the gin was of the rummy-playing variety. Apparently the card game was a nightly ritual between the two, and James was far from the lugubrious character he appeared. That was an act put on for guests as a matter of professional pride.

Certainly Scott seemed eager enough to join him, as he quickly gulped down his coffee, and not for an instant did Sara consider he might have any ulterior motive. In fact, she viewed it as an opportune moment to take her leave.

However, when Scott rose to go, Neville excused himself, too. Evidently he wished to have a private word with the boy, for the rise and fall of their voices could be heard out in the hallway.

Sara stood up in readiness to depart, this time determined to insist on hiring a taxi, even if Dryden offered a lift. Their antagonism might have faded over the meal but, without Scott's presence, she had a feeling it would resurface all too easily, and she would prefer not to ruin what had turned out to be a surprisingly pleasant evening.

When a couple of minutes passed, Sara's eyes began to wander round the room. It wasn't over-cluttered, but the *objets d'art* there were she recognised as being good pieces.

The finest was probably an antique chess set. Laid on a marble table, the figures were carved out of dark and light jade to represent the Mandarin court of old China. She thought of her brother Simon and how much he would have appreciated such a set. An antique-lover, like their father, he was also a chess fanatic.

She was examining the intricate carving on the white Mandarin king when Neville reappeared. She jumped a little guiltily and replaced the figure on its square, while he crossed to stand beside her.

'I think I'd better go. It's getting late,' she said stiltedly—and rather feebly, too, as it was only nine o'clock.

At any rate, he ignored the remark and asked instead, 'Do you play? Or were you merely admiring the set?'

Sara's lips thinned. Was it her imagination or was there the faintest touch of condescension in the question? 'It's very beautiful,' she said coolly, glancing again at the exquisite jade, 'and, as a matter of fact, I do play.'

'Well?' he enquired.

'I know the basic moves. Why?'

'Perhaps we could have a game to help pass the time . . . peaceably at least.'

Very funny, Sara thought grumpily, unable to see why they had to pass any time, peaceably or otherwise. 'I think it would be safer if I just went home,' she responded.

'Probably,' he agreed, 'but, if you do, Scott's going to imagine I've offended you, *again*—and after he has been trusting enough to leave you alone with me. So one game, mm?'

Sara wasn't sure whether he was being mocking or serious, but she supposed Scott might view her departure that way, and she didn't want another argument on her account.

'All right,' she agreed reluctantly, and sat down, while he arranged the chess table between her armchair and the plush leather sofa.

'Would you like some music?' he asked when everything was in position.

'That would be pleasant,' she replied politely, thinking music might cover any lack of conversation.

He crossed to the walnut cabinet which housed a modern hi-fi unit. She left the choice of music to him, and he picked something light and classical. Then, after pouring them both brandies, he relaxed back on the sofa.

'You can start if you like.' His lazy drawl suggested she would probably need every advantage.

Sara decided a little gamesmanship would not go amiss. 'You won't expect too much of me, will you?' she appealed.

He smiled indulgently. 'Don't worry—I won't play for serious.'

'Oh, good.' She smiled nervously, then stared at the board, as if finding an opening move alone was a terrific ordeal.

For a moment she questioned if she was overdoing it. But no—when she glanced up at him he was wearing the patient look of a superior male confronted by the dithering indecision of a female. And, when game commenced, he proceeded to play as though his opponent were a half-wit. Not badly or anything. He simply made his moves with the minimum of thought, and scarcely paid any attention to hers.

In fact, every time Sara looked up, he seemed to be studying her rather than the board. She stared back once, but he was unperturbed. He simply gave her one of his slow, lazy smiles and it was she who ended up looking away in embarrassment.

She'd always wondered what was meant by 'bedroom' eyes. Now she knew. Or had she imagined the thoughts that lay behind his dark blue gaze, the desire conveyed by the sensuous curve of his mouth?

Perhaps she had. Perhaps it was only she who felt... felt what? She shook her head, refusing to give it a name.

'We don't have to play if you don't want,' he said in a soft drawl that suggested other things they might do.

No, she wasn't imagining it, Sara decided, as she raised her head once more and met his eyes. He was a master at it—this other game. And she was...

A fool if she even tried to play it! she told herself sharply, and, in more belligerent mood, reached for her bishop and very purposely annihilated one of his pawns.

'Your move,' she said in a flat voice that denied any intimacy between them.

He seemed unconcerned, smiling still as he brought forward one of his knights, and, while Sara kept her concentration rigidly on the game, he continued to play in the same laidback fashion as before. The last thing he expected was any classic opening plays.

'Check...mate, I think,' Sara murmured after a dozen moves.

'Sorry?' He had already gone back to contemplating the end of his cigar rather than the game.

'Checkmate,' she repeated, and hid a smile—a genuine one this time—as he began to stare in disbelief at the board. 'Do you want me to explain how?'

'No, I see it!' he snapped, his gaze lifting abruptly from the table to her face.

All wide-eyed innocence, she claimed, 'Luck, I suppose.'

For several seconds he looked doubtful enough to be taken in. Then he lowered his eyes back to the board, mentally reconstructing the game to which he'd paid such scant attention, and Sara saw him gradually register the standard play she'd used.

'Amazing,' he finally drawled. 'Do you know you've just managed to reproduce, move for move, a classic opener devised by a Grand Master, no less? I can hardly credit it.'

The irony in his voice told Sara he *didn't* credit it, but she still felt she'd had her revenge for that afternoon's skating 'lesson'.

'I did say I knew some basic moves,' she pointed out.

'So you did,' he conceded with a wry smile, evidently appreciating the joke now he'd recovered from the shock of losing. 'Would you care to risk another game?'

Sara gave a nod, although she doubted she would be allowed to win this one so easily.

'You can go first if you like,' she echoed his earlier words, and he gave her another amused smile, before commencing play.

It was, as she'd anticipated, an entirely different game. This time they played chess and nothing else. When she tried a clever opener, he not only spotted it but almost had her in check with his reply. After that, she concentrated on defence and gradually accepted that she'd need a miracle to win, although she managed to keep blocking his attacks.

'You're good,' he said, no hint of condescension now. 'Do you play regularly?'

'No, not since... since a while. But I was taught by a champion. County, not world,' she stated drily.

'Still quite impressive, I should imagine,' he commented, then, taking his move, added casually, 'Your husband?'

'No, my brother,' she replied, stiffening slightly.

A longer silence followed, and he waited for her next play before he said more directly, 'Do you mind if I ask how long you've been a widow?'

The question wasn't that unusual and was admittedly politer than the way he'd phrased it at the ice rink, so she could hardly avoid it without appearing inordinately sensitive.

'Three and a half years,' she said flatly, hoping that would satisfy his curiosity.

It didn't. 'You're young to be widowed. Did your husband die in an accident?'

'No, from a coronary,' she responded, and steeled herself against the memories evoked.

One perfectly normal summer's day Nick had gone to work at the hospital, and, while actually on casualty duty, had suffered a massive heart attack. It had taken ten minutes to locate another doctor. By that time it had already been too late.

'How old was he?' Neville Dryden's voice brought her back to the present, and she realised he was wondering if there had been a large age gap.

'Thirty-one,' she replied coldly.

He looked surprised. 'Were you aware he had a heart condition?' he asked and, when she shook her head, pursued, 'How long were you married?'

'Three years,' she responded briefly, and again tried to hold back the memories.

They'd had so little time together, she and Nick. They'd spent much of their courtship miles apart and much of their marriage snatching an hour or two between work shifts. They'd put up with it for the promise of a better future and instead they'd been cheated.

It was a bitter thought, made more so as Dryden added carelessly, 'Happily married?'

'I really don't think that's any of your business,' she returned coldly and, knocking over her king, conceded the game to him.

His brows rose at the angry gesture. 'I presume that means you weren't.'

'No, it means—stop being so bloody nosy!' Sara snapped, and got to her feet.

He followed, blocking her path to the door. When she made to brush past him, he caught her arm. She raised her head, the temper in her eyes clashing with the puzzlement in his.

'Let me go!' she spat, but she might have saved her breath.

The fingers gripping her arm tightened at her attempt to pull free. 'Look, I wasn't trying to upset you,' he claimed, impatience in his tone.

'You don't have to *try*,' she threw back.

'Meaning?' he demanded curtly.

'I suspect you have a gift for it,' she retorted, no longer hiding her dislike.

For a moment Neville was more disconcerted than anything else. God, but she was touchy! He asked himself why he was bothering. Surely he knew enough willing women—more beautiful women—without pursuing one who treated him as if he were contagious.

'I suspect you're right,' he finally murmured back, and turned on a smile that usually guaranteed a favourable response.

Even Sara was thrown for an instant. How did you keep arguing with someone when they agreed with you? Or keep scowling at them when they offered you a hundred-watt smile, phoney though it undoubtedly was?

'And I'm sorry for being so "bloody nosy",' he added with a half-amused, half-apologetic look.

Sara frowned. Had she said that to him? She wasn't normally that rude to anyone. She wasn't normally rude, full stop.

'Yes, well, perhaps I was a little abrupt,' she conceded, but in a stiff manner that told him his charm wasn't working. 'Now, could I use your telephone? I'd like to call a taxi.'

'I'll take you home,' came the immediate response.

'There's no need.' Her refusal was just as quick.

'Dammit.' He scowled. 'Are we going to have this conversation every time I offer you a lift?'

The charm had so quickly changed to snapping irritation. The real Neville Dryden, Sara thought, and it was her turn to smile. Somehow she felt she was winning whatever game he was playing.

Definitely winning, although he growled, 'Come on,' and marched her out to the hallway.

After all, he couldn't force her to accept a lift. She'd simply walk up to the main road and hail a taxi.

She shrugged off his hand and waited as he retrieved her coat from the hall-stand. She was just putting it on when Scott reappeared from the kitchen at the back of the house. Evidently, he'd been listening out for them.

'Goodnight, Sara,' he said politely, 'and thanks for going skating with me.'

'I enjoyed it.' She managed a smile for the boy.

'So did I.' He smiled back. 'The concert should be fun too.'

'Concert?' she echoed.

At her obvious mystification, he said to Neville, 'Haven't you asked her yet?'

The man shook his head and forestalled any further discussion by muttering, 'I'm working up to it, OK?'

Sara was left to wonder about the exchange, as he caught her arm and guided her down the steps to the

car. With Scott watching from the doorway, she resigned herself to being driven home. When they pulled
away from the house, she waited for the man to vol-
unteer an explanation of the boy's question.

A full five minutes passed before he said, 'I'm taking
Scott to a concert in a couple of days' time, and he'd
like you to come with us.'

Sara glanced at him in the light of the street lamps
along Chelsea Embankment. His handsome face was set
in disgruntled lines, telling her the invitation had been
extended solely on Scott's behalf. Assuming her refusal
would be taken as read, she lapsed into silent contem-
plation of the dark, misty river.

She was genuinely surprised when he prompted, 'Well,
will you go?'

'No.' She didn't feel it needed qualifying.

Apparently he did. 'Why not?'

Sara thought the reasons should be self-evident. Apart
from her dislike of the man, her presence had already
caused too much friction between him and the boy.

'I don't wish to get involved,' she said flatly.

'With Scott or with me?' he countered.

'With the situation. *You* don't come into it,' she stated.

'Don't I? You were happy enough to go skating with
him.'

'And you were quick enough to warn me off taking
any further interest.'

'I told you I'd changed my mind, remember?' he said
irritably. 'Scott obviously wants your company.'

'And, of course, you always do what Scott wants,'
Sara replied in sceptical tones.

His voice hardened. 'If I can. He may not be deprived
in the same way as the kids with whom you normally
deal—but he's gone through a tough time in the last few
years.'

And where were you? Sara could have asked but she
saw no point. Accusing Dryden of past negligence would

solve nothing and, for better or for worse, the boy needed him now.

She said instead, 'Scott's mother, how did she die?'

'Didn't Scott tell you?' He sounded surprised.

'He said something the first night at the police station, but I thought he might be dramatising.'

'Yes, he does have that tendency at times. What did he say exactly?'

'That she'd killed herself,' she admitted hesitantly, and heard him swear under his breath. 'Is it true?'

'In Scott's eyes, possibly,' he said after consideration. 'She drove headlong into a wall while drunk. Not an unusual condition for Annie, I'm afraid, but I doubt she consciously wrecked herself. Unfortunately, the papers hinted at a connection between the accident and her being axed from her TV series.'

'She was an actress?' Sara was surprised Scott hadn't mentioned the fact.

Dryden nodded. 'That's how we met. We were students together at RADA. She was a good actress, too. Wasted on TV soap. But then things never did go right for Annie,' he finished with a sigh.

Sara frowned, more than a little puzzled by his attitude. He spoke as if he'd cared for Scott's mother, yet he seemed to have no sense of being responsible for at least some of her problems.

She allowed herself a little curiosity. 'What was she like?'

'Beautiful, bright, fun to be around when she was sober,' he relayed, 'vulnerable and rather pathetic when she wasn't.'

'And to Scott?' Sara slipped into her professional role.

'A good mother by anyone's standards. Or at least she was until he was about eight. Then she made a disastrous marriage with an actor, several years her junior. He didn't have a great deal of time for Scott and, after a couple of years, he left Annie with a pile of debts and a drink problem. Perhaps I should have taken him away then, but I couldn't.'

'Because of your work?' Sara assumed he meant.

He shook his head. 'No, I could have made some arrangement there. I just wasn't sure if I had the right to do it. You see, for all her drinking she loved the boy, and he loved her. It was hardly happy families, of course. Often as not, he helped the maid put Annie to bed, and she once arrived at his school fête falling-down-drunk. But he wouldn't leave her, no matter what she did, and I couldn't make him. Though the way things turned out, maybe I should have tried.'

'I don't know.' Experience had taught Sara there was no right or wrong thing in such a situation. 'If you had taken him away, he would have resented you and blamed himself for her death. As it is, if he's angry with anyone, it's with Annie for leaving him, and maybe he'll get over that in time. It's what you do now that's important... Have you sole custody?'

He nodded. 'Yes; only sometimes, when I'm working abroad or my mother's in residence, I have to rely on Pauline, Annie's sister, to look after him.'

'He doesn't seem to like her very much.' Sara recalled Scott's comments on his aunt in Hastings.

'Unfortunately, no,' Neville confirmed. 'I'm afraid she doesn't know how to handle him. He tends to be stubborn and difficult with her, while she expects him to be grateful. The last time I had to bribe her to have him at all... And, like my mother, she's not above reminding him of his illegitimacy.'

'How unfair!' Sara declared.

'Very,' he agreed shortly. 'I take it Scott has revealed his parentage.'

There was a questioning lift to his voice but Sara confined herself to a brief nod when he glanced at her. She found it odd that he didn't realise anyone seeing Scott and him together would have no doubts who had fathered the boy.

'Anyway, between Annie and Pauline, and of course my dear mama,' he continued, 'Scott has become rather contemptuous of the female gender. And I must confess my usual lady-friends haven't done much to alter that. Which is why it might be good for him to spend some time in the company of an intelligent, attractive woman.'

Which was presumably where she came in, Sara thought, taking the flattery with a pinch of salt. Every instinct warned her not to trust Neville Dryden.

'Actually, I haven't noticed Scott has any particular problem in that direction,' she said, just as they pulled up outside her house.

He switched off the engine and, flicking on the interior light, turned in his seat to face her. 'That's because you are an exception—a woman for whom he doesn't have contempt. He even had the nerve to suggest it would be good for *me* to go out with a woman like you.' A slow, amused smile appeared as he added in a murmur, 'Mind you, he may just have a point.'

Too smooth by half, Sara groaned inwardly. Why did she have the feeling Scott's interests were about to take second place to Dryden's inclinations?

'Anyway, you'll come to the concert,' he concluded from her silence.

This time she hesitated fractionally before saying, 'No.'

They came full circle as he asked, 'Why not?'

'Because something tells me it wouldn't be good for me, Mr Dryden,' she stated drily.

It drew another amused smile. 'You're a hard-headed woman, Sara Peters. And you still don't like me very much, do you?' He sounded intrigued rather than offended by the fact.

'Let's just say I don't like being charmed,' Sara replied frankly, then reached for the door handle.

Before she could open it, a hand fastened on her arm to prevent her climbing out. 'All right, you prefer a more direct approach. I'll remember that.'

'Mr Dryden,' Sara clipped back, 'I prefer no approach—direct or indirect. So if I could have my arm back?'

Her request was ignored. In fact, she no longer had his attention, his eyes staring past her towards the house. She turned her head to discover what had distracted him.

The front door was open, light from the hallway outlining Bob, her lodger, as he stood on the step, a couple of empty milk bottles in hand. He'd obviously noticed the strange car parked outside the house and was indulging in a little understandable curiosity.

On recognising Sara, he raised his hand in a brief wave, then placed the milk bottles down before discreetly disappearing inside.

'Is that the reason you're refusing to go to the concert?' Dryden said accusingly and, without giving her a chance to reply, demanded, 'Who is he?'

'My lodger. Not that it's any of your business!' Sara retorted.

'Your lodger?' was echoed in disbelief. 'Why didn't you tell me you were damn well living with a man?'

'You didn't ask,' she replied on a hard, flippant note.

His face darkened to a scowl. 'No, but I assumed——'

'Too bloody much!' she cut in angrily. 'For your information, I don't live *with* Bob. He rents the rooms upstairs, and that's all.'

'Really.' He sounded unconvinced, and his righteous tone had Sara gasping at the hypocrisy of it.

'Yes, *really*! With his wife, Kathy, if you must know,' she threw back.

For a moment he looked at a loss, the dark flush on his handsome face acknowledging the error he'd made. 'I suppose I should apologise...'

'Don't force yourself!' Sara snapped at this offhandedness and, jerking her arm free, yanked open the passenger door.

The move took him by surprise but she heard the slam of his door as she hurried up the pathway. He caught her before she could find her house key and, as he pulled her round to face him, sent her open bag flying. The contents scattered everywhere.

'Now look what you've done!' she almost shouted at him.

'It wasn't deliberate, you know,' he said in his defence, as they both stooped to pick up the clutter she stored in the shoulder-bag.

'I can manage!' Ungraciously she grabbed a hairbrush and packet of tissues from his hand.

But he continued to help, at the same time excusing, 'I just wanted to say I was sorry for jumping to the wrong conclusion.'

'Well, try a little less dramatic method next time,' she suggested with heavy sarcasm.

'All right, I will,' he agreed, *'next time.'*

Sara pulled a face at the last, but muttered a forced, 'Thanks,' after he grubbed around the flower-border to find some loose change and the all-important key.

'About the concert——' he began when they'd stood up again.

'I'm *not* going,' she stated on an emphatic note.

'Fine. But if you were to change your mind, it's not a dress affair,' he went on obliviously. 'So wear something casual. The more downmarket, the better.'

'Why? What kind of concert is it?' she asked, curious despite herself.

'If I tell you that, you definitely won't come,' he replied with a dry laugh.

'I won't anyway,' she reverted to her stubborn stance.

'Perhaps not, but, just in case, we'll call for you about six-thirty, Tuesday evening,' he informed her. Then, as if the whole matter were cut and dried, he sauntered off down the pathway.

'Don't bother! I'll be out!' she threw after him, but to little effect other than his turning to smile at her from the gate.

And, though she'd had the last word this time, Sara was again left seething with frustration.

How did you deal with a man like that?

CHAPTER SIX

SARA spent a restless night, and woke the next morning to the shrill demand of the telephone.

It took some moments to disentangle herself from the bedclothes, stumble towards the living-room, and mutter a rather disgruntled, 'Yes?' into the telephone.

'It's Scott...Scott Collins. I didn't get you out of bed, did I?' an anxious voice asked.

'No, not at all,' Sara lied kindly.

And the boy's voice brightened as he went on, 'Oh, good. Neville thought I should phone at a more civilised hour but I knew *you'd* be up. It's about the concert...'

'Yes?' She wondered what story he'd been told.

'It's just that Neville doesn't seem too sure if you can come or not,' the boy relayed, 'so he suggested I call and check.'

'I see,' Sara said with considerable restraint, while she fumed at Dryden's underhand tactics.

'You can, can't you?' Scott appealed.

'Well...' She paused to find an excuse, but was too slow.

'I honestly think you would enjoy it,' he pursued, 'no matter what Neville might have said. I mean, you're not half as stuffy as he is sometimes.'

'Thank you.' Sara smiled at this backhanded compliment. 'Would I be right in assuming it's a pop concert?'

'Sort of, yes, only I can't tell you who it is, because Neville says you'll run a mile if I do,' the boy confided, before realising he was hardly being encouraging. 'Of

course, his music taste is positively prehistoric,' he added
with disdain.

'Really.' Sara couldn't help laughing at this dismissal
of classical music. In truth, she had little appreciation
of it either.

'You will come, won't you?' Scott's voice changed to
a wheedling note.

And, though the man's charm left her cold, Sara had
no resistance to the boy's. 'All right, you've talked me
into it.'

'Great!' he enthused and, confirming the time they'd
collect her, rang off.

It didn't take long for Sara's agreeable mood to fade,
as she imagined him reporting back to his father. Clearly
Dryden had avoided all mention of last night's quarrel.
Instead he'd got Scott to telephone, knowing she'd have
difficulty refusing him. But why? Was he *really* interested in her?

Sara shook her head at the idea. She was neither
blonde nor beautiful nor dumb enough to suit Neville
Dryden's tastes. If he occasionally flirted with her—in
his lazy, offhand way—then it was probably just to keep
in practice.

No, his real interest was Scott. If the boy had taken
a fancy to a horse or a dog, he'd have bought it for him.
As it was, he'd settled on Sara, so the man was prepared
to put up with her, too.

It was hardly flattering, but Sara supposed it was for-
givable, stemming as it did from a desire to please the
boy. It made her wonder if she'd misjudged him in that
respect. She'd assumed he'd taken responsibility for Scott
because he'd had no other choice, but, if that was the
case, he showed little resentment at the situation. In fact,
to Sara's mind it was the one genuine thing about Neville
Dryden—his affection for his son. Perhaps it really had
been as he'd claimed. Perhaps he'd had to stand on the

sidelines rather than forcibly separate Scott from his mother. Sara could understand that.

What puzzled her was how *he* felt about Annie Collins. He had been generous about her good points and sympathetic about her weaknesses, but at the same time he'd talked of her in an almost impersonal manner. It was as if she'd been a friend, not a lover. Had she just been one in a long list of girls, distinguished only by the fact she'd had his child? Had a younger Annie, deeply in love, hoped to hold him with a baby? Was that what he'd meant by saying things had never worked out for her?

Sara shook her head again, wondering why she was wasting time on such speculation. Whatever had happened between them, it had probably not been to Neville Dryden's credit. But that wasn't her concern. Forget the man and his love life. She would go to the concert because Scott wanted her to and *that was all*.

Decision made, Sara directed her thoughts elsewhere. She looked round her sitting-room, discovered it was even messier than usual and went to change into old jeans and jumper. She didn't much like housework—who did?—but she disliked mess fractionally more.

Her flat seemed to become untidy so easily. Perhaps that was because it lacked adequate space for all her furniture, books and thriving collection of pot-plants. What she now used as a bedroom had originally been an alcoved dining area, and, to accommodate a double bed, wardrobe and chest of drawers, she'd had to shift the table and sideboard into the main lounge. The result was that both rooms were overcrowded, and, somewhat illogically, one had to walk through the bedroom to reach the kitchen.

On the whole, however, she did not regret subletting the house. It was her father who had bullied her into doing so. Worried about her living alone in London, he'd suggested she share the whole house with another girl. Sara had felt that would leave her too little privacy, and instead she'd turned the smallest bedroom upstairs into a kitchen, making the two floors self-contained apart from the use of the bathroom.

Then she'd casually mentioned the conversion at work, and Bob, who had been desperate to get out of a couple of seedy rooms in Wandsworth, had virtually begged her for the top flat.

At first she'd had reservations about renting to him. Like selling a car, it seemed the fastest way of losing a friend. But, fortunately, it had worked out well.

The couple were ideal tenants, Bob taking over responsibility for the garden while his wife kept their flat spotless. If they often had people round for a meal, they were very considerate about noise levels. And she'd gained a new friend in his wife, Kathy.

In fact, it was Kathy who later came downstairs to invite her for a rather late Christmas lunch. Yet to stock up her fridge, Sara had readily accepted the invitation.

During the meal, they talked of Bob and Kathy's Christmas, spent between their respective families in Yorkshire, and the various mishaps, insults and arguments that had ensued. Sara was a good listener and it was only at the end that Kathy realised they'd monopolised the conversation. To make up for it, she asked Sara how her Christmas had been.

'Quiet but enjoyable,' Sara summed up.

'No wild parties?' teased Bob.

'No, not unless you count my parents' Christmas Eve dinner.' Her wry look suggested it could hardly be termed wild.

Kathy still asked, 'What was your partner like this time?'

Sara gave a shrug, and, with obvious disinterest, relayed, 'He was a colleague of my brother's—reasonably pleasant in a serious sort of way.'

'She means he was deadly dull,' Kathy interpreted for Bob's benefit.

A rather accurate interpretation, and Sara had to laugh. 'Well, not deadly. Let's just say I know a whole lot more about micro-surgery than I used to.'

Kathy rolled her eyes. '*That* was his dinner-table conversation!'

Sara nodded. 'To be fair, I was partly to blame. You see, after we'd exhausted the miserable weather, the shocking house prices in Kent and the even more shocking house prices in London, he was so obviously scrabbling round for conversation that I asked him about his work.'

'Always fatal with a man,' Kathy groaned in sympathy. 'I'm surprised all that micro-surgery didn't put you off your meal.'

'It really was quite interesting,' Sara said more charitably. 'And he only talked so much because he was shy.'

To this apparent paradox, Kathy conceded, 'I suppose that does make some convoluted sense.'

'How old was he?' Bob chipped in.

Sara paused for consideration. 'I'm not sure. Mid-thirties, possibly.'

'That wasn't him last night, was it?' Kathy caught on to what her husband was already wondering.

'Last night?' Sara's thoughts were still focused on Paul Cartwright.

Humorously, the other girl explained, 'The tall dark stranger following you up the garden path.'

Sara's expression stiffened then, as the harmless image of her brother's friend was supplanted by the infinitely more disturbing one of Neville Dryden.

'Kathy here just happened to be peering casually out of the window at the time,' Bob revealed.

'Very funny!' His wife gave him a sour look, then suggested meaningfully, 'Isn't there something you want to watch on the bedroom telly?'

'Not to my knowledge, but I can take a hint.' Bob rose from the table and, before disappearing, winked at Sara. 'Scream for help if she brings out the thumbscrews.'

Sara laughed, but his wife was less amused, muttering, 'Sometimes I could cheerfully strangle him.'

'He doesn't mean anything,' appeased Sara.

'Doesn't he?' Kathy pulled a face. 'You know, the worst of it is, he's right. I am pretty nosy, aren't I?'

'I wouldn't say that,' Sara responded.

'Only because you're too polite to,' Kathy said, smile reappearing for a moment, before she announced rather grandly, 'Well, for once I'm going to be the soul of discretion and not ask any more questions about your doctor friend.'

Of course, Sara could have left it like that. She was tempted. But, in a way, it would be tantamount to lying.

'Actually, the man you saw last night wasn't my dinner partner,' she admitted, and Kathy took it as an invitation to show interest.

'Really? Come to think of it, he didn't look your staid, serious type.'

'*That* he's not!' Sara agreed with emphasis, then felt almost obliged to go on, 'You remember the actor I mentioned last week—the one I ran into at Fulham Police Station?'

'The thoroughly obnoxious individual?' Kathy quoted Sara's description at the time.

'The same,' she confirmed.

'Heavens, how did you meet him again?' Kathy said, before answering the question herself, 'I know—the boy who called yesterday.'

'Yes, that's his . . . his ward, Scott.' Sara decided not to go into the real relationship between the two.

'Bob said the boy seemed very disappointed you weren't here. Was he in some sort of trouble?' Kathy asked, sympathetic now rather than curious.

'Not really.' Sara gave an edited account of the family quarrel and subsequent events, this time referring to the actor by his name.

'Dryden?' Kathy repeated. 'You don't mean Neville Dryden, do you?'

'Unfortunately.' Sara nodded back.

'Why, he's famous! And you said I wouldn't have heard of him,' Kathy accused.

'*I* hadn't.' Sara shrugged back.

'Honestly?' Kathy clearly viewed this ignorance as little short of amazing. 'He's been in some marvellous TV plays.'

'I don't have a TV,' Sara pointed out.

'Films, then?' Kathy pursued. 'I mean, the newspapers rate him as one of the best young actors in British cinema today.'

Sara remained unimpressed, generally sceptical about anything printed in the popular Press. 'Well, the "young" is an exaggeration for a start.'

'Why? How old is he?' Kathy quizzed.

'I don't know. Nudging forty, perhaps,' Sara suggested rather unfairly.

'He didn't look it. Mind you, I only got a glance of him as he walked up the path. And I *really* wasn't spying on you,' Kathy stressed. 'It's just that Bob came upstairs, raving about the classy car you'd arrived home in.'

'Don't worry,' Sara smiled, 'I'd probably have done some curtain-twitching myself.'

'Not you. You're the least curious person I know.'

'Some of the parents on my case-load wouldn't agree with that.'

Married to a social worker, Kathy understood this dry comment. 'Yes, Bob says he's frequently told to mind his own business. Personally, I couldn't put up with the kind of abuse you get.'

Sara shrugged. 'I would have thought you'd come in for a fair bit as a teacher.'

'Maybe,' Kathy conceded, 'but at least I don't have to visit the ghastly kids' even more ghastly parents.'

Sara laughed at this exaggeration. She knew in reality Kathy cared about the children she taught, especially the ones from difficult homes. If she lacked sympathy, it was for the parents who caused the neglect. And Sara could hardly criticise her for that. At times she found her own tolerance strained to the limits.

'It's not so bad,' she finally said, meaning to close the subject, and, indicating the debris of lunch, went on, 'I'll give you a hand with the washing-up.'

The two women worked as a team, clearing the table and carrying the dishes through to the adjoining kitchen, before Kathy washed and Sara dried.

They were immersed in the task when Kathy suddenly asked, 'So what's he like?'

'Who?'

'Neville Dryden, of course.'

'Oh, him.' Sara shrugged indifference.

'So blasé. Anyone would think you spent your life hobnobbing with the rich and famous,' Kathy said on a dry note, then slipped in, 'I take it he is.'

'Is what?'

'Rich.'

'Filthy, I should imagine.'

'What more could a girl ask for?' Kathy appealed of no one in particular but directing a speculative glance at Sara.

'Uh-uh. If you're thinking what I think you're thinking, forget it.'

'Why?'

'*Why?*' Sara echoed in disbelief. 'You mean, besides the fact that he's arrogant, conceited and *the* most irritating man I've ever met?'

This catalogue of faults should have been enough to convey her feelings towards Neville Dryden, but Kathy still came back with, 'Well, he doesn't sound dull, at any rate.'

Sara had to laugh, 'No, I'll give him that. Dull he isn't.'

'And, personality apart, don't you find all that dark, brooding masculinity the teeniest weeniest bit attractive?' Kathy persisted.

'Not in the least,' Sara denied, meaning it, and, once again, moved the conversation on to a different topic.

But an echo of Kathy's words returned the next evening when she opened the door to Neville Dryden. He was dressed in black cords and a worn leather jacket, with his face shadowed by an even darker growth of beard, but somehow he managed to look just as handsome as the first night they'd met. And, for a moment, Sara wondered how honest she was being. Didn't a small part of her, a wholly feminine part, respond to the sheer masculinity of the man?

Then he smiled, a slow, lazy smile, and she told herself she had to be crazy thinking that way at all.

She lowered her gaze to the object he was carrying, and proceeded to stare at it somewhat warily.

'It's a cactus,' he stated the obvious.

'Yes, I *had* realised.'

'We thought you might not be the flower type,' he added.

Sara frowned, not quite sure how to take this. Presumably he was in the habit of bringing his girlfriends flowers. And what did she rate? A fat, round, prickly cactus. Was it meant to represent *her* type?

'Thank you,' she said with bare civility as he handed her the bowl, 'but you didn't have to bother.'

'No bother. Regard it as a peace offering,' he suggested, smile now wry.

For what? Sara might have asked, considering a multitude of offences it could cover, but she confined herself to giving him a sceptical look. Then she retreated to put his gift into her flat and collect her jacket.

The jacket was tailored, in tan suede, but the rest of her outfit of jeans and check shirt was very casual. When she returned to the door, Dryden awarded her a once-over appraisal, possibly comparing her with his more glamorous lady-friends.

Lips pursed, Sara wondered how long their truce would last. All of ten minutes, she suspected, unless they both made an effort in front of Scott.

He was waiting for them in the car, relegated to the back seat. She might have joined him there if the front passenger door hadn't been ceremoniously opened for her.

When she climbed in, the boy leaned forward between the front seats and asked, in greeting, 'What did you think of the cactus?'

'Very nice.' She smiled. 'I haven't seen one quite that variety before.'

Scott looked pleased at her approval. 'The man in the shop said it was pretty rare, and I knew you'd like it better than the soppy flowers Neville wanted to buy. That's what he usually gives his *dumb* girlfriends,' he confided, regardless of the fact that the driver's seat was now occupied.

It made Dryden turn round and enquire, 'Has anyone ever told you, squirt, that you talk too much?'

Uncrushed, Scott relayed with a grin, 'So far: my Aunt Pauline, your mother, the PE instructor at my last school, the physics master at my present one—and you, on numerous occasions.'

'Obviously to no effect.' Dryden shook his head in exasperation and turned back to start the car.

When they'd pulled away from the pavement, Scott went on, 'It's a sign of a highly active brain, you know.'

'Hmm.' A sceptical sound from Dryden. 'Then it's a pity this highly active brain doesn't manifest itself in other ways, isn't it?'

Again Scott didn't seem offended, explaining to Sara, 'That's a dig against my end-of-term report. He just read it today.'

'Only because I didn't want to spoil my Christmas,' Dryden groaned.

'Not good?' Sara surmised.

'Well...' Scott hesitated before saying, 'Mr Clarkson, my English teacher, thinks I have natural literary and dramatic ability.'

'That's complimentary enough,' Sara commented, although she suspected it might not be the full story.

It wasn't, as Dryden pointed out. 'Unfortunately his other masters found nine different ways to say he was bright but lazy.'

'A couple of them thought I was trying,' Scott added in his defence.

Dryden gave a short laugh. 'I'd agree with that, squirt.'

'Funny.' Scott pulled a face.

Sara kept silent but her sympathy was with the boy.

He showed no signs of being deflated, bouncing back with, 'I bet you weren't so brilliant at school, either.'

'Then you'd lose your money,' Dryden claimed. 'Modesty alone forbids me from telling you *how* brilliant.'

Sara decided he couldn't possibly be serious, even before she caught his amused look. Like Scott, she was willing to bet, too, that he'd been nobody's idea of a star pupil. Very bright, possibly, but not a conformist.

'Well, you'll see,' Scott rallied. 'I'll be just as brilliant when I transfer to Hilliard's.'

'Hilliard's?' Sara glanced round in surprise. 'You mean the arts school in Kensington?'

Scott nodded, then went on to explain, 'Neville's promised that after summer term I can come and live in

London all the time. And, as I'm not much good at games and hopeless at science, he thinks I'd be better off at a school like Hilliard's. What do you think?' he asked, his tone willing her to agree.

'From what I've heard, I'm sure you'll enjoy it more,' Sara said, knowing that the school, if unconventional, was reputed to provide an excellent arts-biased education. But she remained surprised by the whole idea. Surely having Scott on a permanent basis would cramp Dryden's style?

Yet he seemed happy enough, smiling as he said, 'And who knows—it might teach him some musical appreciation.'

'I already have some,' Scott retorted smartly. 'It just happens to be different from yours.'

To this, Dryden gave another groan and asked of Sara, 'Has he told you whom we're going to see tonight?'

'Not yet,' she replied.

'Well, I don't expect you'll be any the wiser,' he continued in a dry tone, 'but they're called Hard Luck, and believe me, the name says it all.'

Scott directed a look at Sara that said, What did I tell you? Stuffy, and she couldn't resist taking his side.

'As a matter of fact, I have heard of them. A lot of people regard them as successors to Led Zeppelin,' she stated knowledgeably.

It drew an admiring grin from the boy and an incredulous glance from the man.

'You don't actually *like* that sort of thing, do you?' The question implied no one with taste could possibly do so.

'Never listen to anything else,' Sara said, quite untruthfully.

Scott realised it, having leafed through her varied record collection, and stifled a laugh.

'You're joking,' came from Dryden, but he looked none too certain of it.

'This is where he starts muttering about bloody Philistines,' Scott confided to Sara.

But the man limited himself to a disgruntled, 'Watch your language!'

'I'm just quoting you,' the boy pointed out.

'Well, don't!' he was told. 'Some people already consider me a doubtful influence on you.'

Some people, Sara took to be a reference to herself, but she resisted rising to the bait. It was going to be a long enough evening.

The traffic increased as they neared Albert Hall, where the concert was to be held, and eventually Dryden deposited them in front of the building before going to find a parking space.

He'd handed Sara two of the three tickets so they could go inside rather than wait for him in the chilly December evening. They were directed to seats in the upper circle, commanding a central view of the stage.

Without knowing the number of the missing ticket, Sara plumped for the seat on Scott's left. It was only when the row filled up that she realised she'd made the wrong choice, and Dryden's seat was next to her rather than Scott.

He materialised just as the concert was due to start, cutting it so fine that Scott said, 'We were beginning to worry you'd run out on us.'

'The thought occurred, I must admit,' the man drawled back.

The boy laughed, taking it as a joke. Sara, however, had her doubts, especially when the curtain parted to reveal the support group, TCP, and Dryden slumped in his seat with an expression best described as martyred.

It prompted her to say, 'They won't be *that* bad,' only to receive a sceptical look in return.

And, after the band played a couple of numbers, she began wishing she'd kept quiet. For it had to be faced—they were most definitely *that* bad.

Loud, grating and discordant, their performance lasted a mercifully brief half-hour, and Scott summed it up in two words. 'They stank!'

'There's hope for you yet, squirt.' Dryden smiled approval of the criticism, then asked of Sara, 'Are you *sure* you like this sort of music?'

'They're not exactly typical,' she found herself defending, though why she should, heaven alone knew. After all, *she* hadn't dragged *him* to the concert!

'Hard Luck will be heaps better,' Scott declared.

'True,' Dryden conceded unexpectedly, before qualifying, 'At least one assumes they couldn't possibly be any worse.'

The sarcasm made Scott groan. 'Your trouble is your age.'

'My age?' the man challenged. 'What's that got to do with it?'

'Well, no offence intended,' the boy assured before going on to give it, 'but you're probably too old to appreciate rock music.'

Sara caught her breath, imagining that Dryden, as an actor, would be more than a little sensitive about his advancing years. She turned out to be quite wrong.

He merely echoed in wry agreement, 'Probably.'

Still, Scott hastened to add, 'Not that I'm saying you *are* old or anything. Just that you have to be pretty young to enjoy it...don't you, Sara?' he appealed for her support.

Presumably this meant she was on the right side of the generation gap, and Sara couldn't resist a sly dig at the man. 'Oh, I don't know...some of the most famous rock stars are over forty.'

'Which I'm not,' came the dry rejoinder, 'despite the impression Superbrat has been trying to give to the contrary.'

'No, I haven't!' Scott protested, then immediately repeated the crime by saying, 'He is nearly, though. I mean he's thirty-seven.'

'And getting older by the second,' Dryden complained.

Scott just smiled, but he took the hint and switched to asking Sara if she'd watched a film screened on Boxing Day television. She hadn't, and so, apparently, had deprived herself of the pleasure of seeing Neville Dryden in action. The film had been based on an Agatha Christie, with several famous celebrities appearing in cameo roles. They, however, were damned with faint praise by Scott.

Sara couldn't help commenting, 'It sounds as if Neville was the single redeeming feature.'

'Pretty much,' the boy agreed, not conscious of any irony.

The man could hardly miss it. Laughing, he confessed, 'What squirt's omitted to tell you is that I only appeared in the first fifteen minutes of the film. Which is perfectly understandable, considering I was the murder victim.'

Sara found herself laughing, too, and wondered if she hadn't misjudged the man. At least he wasn't overconceited about his acting talents.

It was Scott who insisted, 'He was still the best, though.'

'Loyal to the last,' Neville approved, drawing a pleased look in reply. 'And who am I to argue? Truth to tell, I made a marvellous corpse.'

'I'm sure you did,' Sara declared, face deadpan.

It had Dryden slanting her a suspicious, if amused, glance. 'You know, I'm not so sure how to take that.'

'I was just agreeing with you,' she pointed out, all innocence.

'She was,' Scott confirmed, hiding a grin.

'A bit of advice, squirt,' Dryden said in dry warning. 'When a woman starts agreeing with you, beware!'

'Of what?' Scott asked.

A good question, Sara thought, also training her eyes on Dryden, as she dared him to continue.

Catching her expression, he seemed to decide better of it, shrugging instead. 'I'll tell you when you're older.'

'As usual,' Scott sighed, and confided to Sara, 'I'll be able to write an encyclopaedia on the things he's going to tell me when I'm older.'

Sara laughed in response, while Dryden countered, 'That's always assuming he can spell by that time.'

It drew an affronted look from Scott, but he didn't get the chance to argue back as the house lights dimmed, signalling the restart of the concert.

From the outset, Hard Luck's superiority was unquestionable. When the curtains parted, the group launched into one of their major hits and drew a roar of approval from the audience, while the lead singer, flamboyant in satin trousers and shirt slashed to the waist, strutted about the stage, camping it up with the confidence of a mega-star.

Of course, they could hardly go wrong. Every song was familiar to dedicated fans and that alone guaranteed a wildly enthusiastic reception. But the lead singer also had a good voice, proving it after several fast rock numbers by switching to a ballad that brought a breathless hush to the hall. And though, in reality, Sara was not a passionate fan of the band, this particular song stirred memories for her, too.

It had been played constantly on the radio the summer she was first married, and, despite the sadness of the lyrics, she was reminded of happier days. Of Nick and her, at the beginning of a lifetime together, making love and making plans, looking forward to a future they would never share.

Sara shut her eyes, bringing herself back to the present before her thoughts could stray further. Perhaps it was a weakness, but she still cried over Nick's death. At times, she couldn't control the impulse, and, sensing Dryden was watching her rather than the stage, the last thing she wanted was to dissolve into tears.

He'd probably have put it down to the song, which he dismissed as, 'Pure schmaltz.'

It was a comment that annoyed Sara immensely, and, echoing Scott, she retorted, 'You know your trouble?'

'Don't tell me.' He ignored her obvious irritation and pretended it was a guessing game. 'I'm too old—right?'

'No, just too damn——' Sara broke off to search for the appropriate word.

'Hard? Cynical? Unfeeling?' he suggested, all in the same amused undertone.

Sara didn't waste breath replying. Clearly, he was quite aware what she thought of him.

She turned away and, during the rest of the concert, stared rigidly ahead. The fact she was ignoring him, however, seemed to go unnoticed as he continued to make the occasional humorous aside until gradually she began waiting for them, schooling her features not to betray the slightest sign of amusement. For she had the feeling that, if discouraging Neville Dryden was proving virtually impossible, then *en*couraging him would be all too easy.

On the drive home, she acted in a similar fashion, limiting any remarks to Scott.

He was full of the concert. Hard Luck, it seemed, rated every superlative in the book.

It was some time before he exhausted the subject and switched to talking about his skiing trip to Switzerland. Though he'd mentioned it earlier, Sara hadn't understood he was due to leave the following day. Now that she did, she felt sorry this would be their last meeting.

When they finally drew up some yards from her gate, she smiled at him. 'Well, don't go breaking any legs.'

'I won't.' He grinned back. 'I'll send you a postcard if you like.'

'That would be nice,' she agreed and, deciding a kiss might be considered soppy, offered her hand.

He shook it, pleased at the adult gesture, then ran on, 'Maybe I'll see you at half-term. I mean if you and Neville are still...sort of friends.'

Understandably, Sara was stuck for a reply. She could hardly point out that she and Neville Dryden had never begun to be friends—sort of or otherwise.

But the man responded, 'Who knows, squirt? Stranger things have happened.' And, mockery plain, he smiled at Sara. 'Well, Mrs Peters, in the interest of friendship, I think I should escort you to your door.'

'Don't bother, it's only a couple of——' she tried to protest, but was left talking to thin air as he climbed out of the car.

Sighing in exasperation, she turned back to the boy. He was grinning broadly, approval all too obvious. It seemed rather late to disillusion him about her feelings towards his father, so she just shook her head, hoping he'd understand.

Then she advised quietly, 'Look after yourself, Scott,' and stepped out of the car.

Having said her farewells to the boy, she did not linger, but setting a fast pace along the pavement did not shake Dryden off. When they reached the lit porchway of her house, he waited patiently while she found the door key.

'Well, goodnight...and thanks,' she eventually mumbled, trusting he'd take the hint and leave.

Instead he said, 'I suppose you're already booked up Friday.'

'Friday?' she echoed. The day's significance was lost on her.

'New Year's Eve,' he reminded with a wry smile.

'Oh.' She'd actually forgotten it was only three days away.

'No plans,' he concluded without giving her a chance to say otherwise. 'In that case, you'll be able to come to a party.'

'With you?' Incredulity made her stupid.

'That was the general idea, yes,' he drawled back.

'But Scott's off to Switzerland tomorrow,' she pointed out.

'So?' he said, shrugging.

Sara's mouth tightened. She felt it plain enough what she'd meant: that there was no need to keep up any pretence of friendship when the boy wasn't around to witness it.

'I thought we might be daring and try a date, without a chaperon,' he explained in amused tones.

Sara gave him a distinctly *un*amused look in reply.

Yet he still continued, 'So you'll come, then.'

'No,' she stated flatly.

'Why not?' he pursued.

Sara stared at him in disbelief. Could he really be that oblivious to her dislike of him? With his ego, she supposed he might be. She searched for a simple excuse. 'I'm afraid my brother is throwing a party the same night,' she said, regardless of the fact she'd not planned on attending it, either.

Undaunted, Dryden came back, 'That's all right. I don't mind going to it instead.'

At first, Sara was thrown by the suggestion. Then, surprisingly, it struck her as funny. How amazed her family would be if she turned up with a partner in tow. And, considering the partner, how appalled, too. But at least it might prove she was capable of finding her own man, if she chose.

She was actually contemplating the idea when she caught the hint of satisfaction in Neville Dryden's smile, and common sense prevailed.

'That wasn't an invitation,' she stated bluntly.

'Wasn't it?' he echoed, feigning surprise. 'How presumptuous of me!'

'Very,' she agreed shortly.

'You're not going with anyone else, though…are you?' he continued.

'No,' she admitted through gritted teeth, 'but that doesn't mean I'm desperate.'

'And should I take it you'd have to be,' he pursued, smile still firmly in place, 'before you went out with me, that is?'

Sara felt he was almost begging to be insulted, but she resisted the temptation. Instead she shrugged, leaving him to draw his own conclusions.

'Oh, don't spare my feelings,' he drawled. 'I mean, you haven't up to now.'

It was then Sara's temper finally snapped. 'All right, if you must know, I think I'd have to be wrong in the head before I went out with an arrogant, self-centred womaniser, who, in my opinion, hasn't any feelings *to* spare! Satisfied?'

She ended on an angry, strident note, resounding in the silence that followed—an interminable silence, as they stared at one another, the bright gleam of defiance in her eyes, something dark and unfathomable in his.

'In that case,' he eventually ground out, 'perhaps it's time I started living up to your expectations.'

At first, Sara didn't realise what he meant. She just stood there as he came a step nearer, closing the gap between them. Just stood there until it was too late to avoid the arms reaching out for her, dragging her body to his.

Of course she should have reacted instinctively, pushed him away or at least tried to. She should have struck out or turned her head—done anything to evade the mouth seeking hers. Yet she did nothing, not even cry out.

How long had it been since she was last held like this, last kissed? So long she'd all but forgotten how it felt. Forgotten the rough sensuality of a man's arms, the hard warmth of a body close to hers. And, in remembering, present merged with past until it ceased to matter who was holding her, kissing her, bringing back bittersweet memories of passion once shared.

Lost in such memories, Sara was barely aware of the man she was with. It wasn't his face she saw when she closed her eyes, wasn't his lips she imagined on hers, his arms she felt round her. She was just using him.

It was a dangerous game to play, especially when Neville Dryden could not be expected to know the rules. All he knew and felt was her response to him, and the sweet surprise of it made him groan in satisfaction. Made control slip away as his mouth opened hungrily on hers, betraying need and desire, demanding the same in return.

Dream suddenly became reality for Sara. Too vivid a reality, too intimate to allow pretence. Now, wholly conscious of who was kissing her in that half-savage, half-loving way, she twisted her head from his.

Free for a moment, her lips formed a cry of protest, but it came out as a small gasping sound that went unheard or ignored, as his hand lifted, fingers grasping her hair, tilting her head back, while his mouth sought hers once more.

Only this time, when he kissed her, it was so different. Soft and persuasive, gently coaxing, as if he knew he'd scared her. She still resisted, straining against his hold, but it was small wonder he took no notice of her struggles, which were growing weaker and more halfhearted by the second, dying away as desire proved stronger than shame or fear. When his lips eventually left hers to trail down the soft nape of her neck, it was she who clung to him, giving an involuntary moan of pleasure.

'God, I want you, Sara Peters,' he groaned in response, and proved how much as he pulled the curve of her hips to his.

The action sent a shudder through Sara's body, a wave of physical longing that was almost pain, and, shocked by the force of it, she pushed away from him.

For a moment he looked confused, trying to understand her erratic behaviour, then he lifted a hand, briefly touching her cheek as he murmured, 'It's all right. I can wait.'

There was an odd gentleness in the gesture that, if anything, added to Sara's distress. Plainly he didn't understand, but how could she admit the desire he'd roused wasn't for him—would never be for him?

She remained frozen as he leaned forward to brush her cold lips with the warmth of his, saying softly, 'I knew it would be like this.'

She searched for the right words to tell him how wrong he was, to explain that it had all been sham on her part. But the words wouldn't come and in the end she lost the chance. With the promise to call on New Year's Eve, he gave her a last smile and walked back up the path to the gate.

He did not turn, and Sara was left staring after him, once again wondering how one dealt with a man like Neville Dryden. Only this time there was more fear than anger in the question. For she knew now he could turn her life upside-down, if she let him.

Still shaken, she entered the house and flat and went straight to her bedroom. She picked up the photograph that rested there, on the bedside table, and lovingly fingered the glass.

But even that didn't work. Though Nick's image was before her, her thoughts and feelings were centred elsewhere. She looked at the thin, sensitive face of her husband and tried to recall how it had been with him. How she'd felt the first time they'd kissed. Had her lips felt the touch of his so long afterwards? Had her heart beat this hard?

She kept staring at the photograph, but for once the memories wouldn't come. And the guilt was crippling. In responding to another man, she believed she'd betrayed Nick just as much as if he'd been alive.

'I still love you,' she said aloud, truly meaning the words.

But it seemed there was no magic in them any more and no answering echo to help her bear the loneliness.

She lay down, holding the picture to her breast, and wept softly, for another part of Nick had died that night.

CHAPTER SEVEN

By New Year's Eve, Sara felt she had things in their proper perspective. What had happened two nights ago she'd put down to a momentary madness, and, in the sanity of daylight, dismissed her fears as irrational.

After all, Neville Dryden couldn't force her to go out with him. She just had to make it plain she didn't want to. The plainer the better, she thought, considering his talent for twisting words to suit him. So she rehearsed a simple flat refusal that could not be construed as anything else, and waited for him to call.

She was still waiting at midday when the doorbell rang. Thinking it might be him in person, she went to the front window and peered round the net curtains, but it was just her brother, smiling quizzically as he noticed her spying on him.

When she opened the door to him, he said, 'You look as though you were expecting somebody else and I came as a severe disappointment.'

'Don't be silly,' she replied a little crossly. 'I was surprised to see you, that's all. I imagined you'd be busy preparing for the party tonight.'

'I am in a way,' he claimed, following her into the flat. 'Marge sent me up to buy some special pâté from Selfridges's, and I thought, as I was here, I'd stop off and say hello.'

'Well, it's nice to see you,' Sara said more pleasantly, and waved him into an armchair. 'Can you stop for lunch?'

'I'd love to, but Marge is presently waging a war against middle-age spread.'

'*Marge* is?'

'Mine, not hers,' her brother explained, his wife being extremely slim. 'I have to fast until the party buffet... Speaking of which, I hope you've changed your mind?'

Sara shook her head. 'Thanks, but no thanks.'

'Oh, come on, Sis,' Simon cajoled. 'It's New Year's Eve. You can't celebrate it by yourself.'

This time Sara gave a shrug. It didn't bother her to be alone. She hadn't planned on celebrating, anyway.

'And I—um—half promised Paul you'd be there,' Simon added hesitantly.

'Paul?' Sara's mind was blank for a moment. 'Oh, you mean your doctor friend.'

He nodded. 'It seems you made a big hit with him at Christmas.'

Had she? Sara was doubtful. As far as she recalled she'd hardly opened her mouth. Of course, with some men that was a virtue in itself.

'Well, I'm afraid he'll have to be disappointed,' she said with a distinct touch of irony.

Hearing it, her brother gave her a reproachful glance. 'I thought you liked him.'

But if he was trying to make Sara feel guilty, he didn't succeed. 'I like lots of people,' she pointed out, 'but that doesn't mean I want to be stuck with them for a whole evening—and certainly not if it entails listening to a lecture on heart disease.'

'That's what he talked about?' her brother said in disbelief.

'Oh, only during the main course,' she admitted. 'By dessert, he'd moved on to laser-surgery.'

Simon frowned, but not in sympathy with her. 'Poor Paul, he's not normally so one-track. You must have made him nervous.'

'Thanks, brother dear.' Sara pulled a face, and was unable to resist a sarcastic, 'Would that be before or after I scored this big hit with him?'

Her brother looked annoyed for a second, then decided to laugh, recognising he was flogging a dead horse. 'All right, forget Paul. Come to the party anyway.'

'No.'

'Why not?'

Sara held a sigh. 'I just don't want to—OK?'

'That's hardly a reason,' Simon grumbled.

'All right,' she retorted in exasperation. 'If you must know, I already have a date.'

'A *date*?' he echoed rather stupidly. 'You mean with a man?'

'Of course!' she snapped, irritated by his gaping stare. Did he really imagine her incapable of finding a man for herself?

'Who?' His eyes narrowed as if he suspected her of lying.

She supposed she was, in a sense, considering her date had failed to call, but he *had* asked her out, so it wasn't altogether a lie.

'You don't know him,' she hedged.

Simon wasn't discouraged. 'What's his name?'

'Dryden,' she admitted briefly.

'That's unusual,' he commented. 'Dryden what?'

Sara began to wish she'd kept quiet. She felt obliged to correct, 'It's *what* Dryden... Neville, to be exact.'

'Neville Dryden,' her brother repeated thoughtfully. 'Funny, it sounds awfully familiar. Is he in the profession?'

'No, he's not.' Sara lifted mental eyebrows at the idea of Neville Dryden being a doctor.

'What does he do, then?' Simon pursued.

She hesitated, realising that if she identified the actor it would only lead to more questions. 'Well, at the moment I believe he's between jobs,' she finally said, another half-truth.

'Oh.' Simon Summerfield was plainly disappointed. 'Between jobs' he took to be a euphemism for unemployed. 'He's not one for your cases, is he?'

'Considering none of them is over eighteen, it's hardly likely,' Sara replied.

It drew a grimace from her brother. 'Come on, Sis, you know what I mean. Is he the father of one of your delinquents?'

Sara could easily have said no. Scott was hardly a delinquent, after all. But she resented her brother's imperious air.

She shrugged instead. 'What if he is?'

'Oh, Sara.' He sighed heavily. 'You can do better than that. It's one thing helping these people, but getting personally involved...' He shook his head at the idea, before another occurred. 'If he's unemployed, what does he do for money? You haven't been loaning him any, have you?'

'What?' Sara frowned at her brother's imaginings, then laughed aloud at the idea of Neville Dryden's borrowing money from her. He was probably richer than her whole family put together. 'No, of course not. If you must know, he doesn't need to work. He's independently wealthy, as they say.'

'Really.' Simon looked no happier at this information.

Sara was beginning to suspect that no man was going to meet his approval—not unless he'd been picked by Simon himself. Obviously he didn't trust her judgement. He'd trust it even less, too, if he ever met Neville Dryden.

When he said, 'Why don't you take him along to the party tonight?' Sara didn't need time to think about it.

'And subject him to the third degree? No, thanks,' she said in a wry tone.

Simon looked offended for a second, then decided to take it in good humour. 'All right, I was being inquisitive. But you can't blame me, Sis. He must be something special, this Dryden fellow.'

'Special' wasn't quite the word Sara would have used, but she let it pass, and, before Simon could probe further, she rose to make coffee.

The kitchen was at the back of the house, accessed via the hall, and she left Simon reading a magazine, while she prepared sandwiches for her own lunch. She was just finishing the task when she heard her phone ringing. She carried the tray of coffee things through to the lounge to find her brother answering it.

'Here she is now, in fact,' he said to the caller, and, waiting for her to deposit the tray on a table, held out the receiver. '"Just tell her it's Neville",' he relayed with a mocking, elder-brother-type smile.

Sara's face fell in response. It was a strain talking to Neville Dryden normally, far less with her brother in audience.

'Yes?' she muttered rather abruptly into the phone.

'Sara?' a voice said with some uncertainty.

'Speaking.'

'It's Neville.'

'Yes, I know.'

Sara did not add to this reply, and for a moment there was silence. Only later did she realise her coldness must have come as a surprise to Neville. After all, she'd been anything but cold when they'd parted two nights ago.

'Who's that?' he finally asked, his tone hardening.

'Pardon?' Sara wasn't ready for the sudden switch.

'The man who answered the phone—who is he?'

'Just my brother.'

'Your brother?' Neville repeated with no attempt to hide his disbelief.

It had Sara muttering, 'Well, so my parents told me.'

The sarcasm drew another silence, then he surprised her by apologising. 'OK, I'm sorry. It's just that you don't seem too pleased by my call... You're not annoyed that I didn't phone earlier, are you?'

'No, of course not. To be honest, I forgot all about it,' Sara claimed with an indifference intended to put him in his place.

It didn't succeed, as he returned, 'Not about the party, I hope. I'll pick you up at nine, all right?'

Now was obviously the time for that simple flat refusal she'd rehearsed. At least, it would have been, had her brother not been sitting opposite her and making no bones about the fact he was listening to their conversation. Caught by her earlier lies about a 'date,' what could she say?

And Neville didn't really wait for a reply, as he ran on, 'By the way, the party is a rather glamorous affair, if you know what I mean.'

Sara gritted her teeth. She knew what he meant all right. Clearly he didn't trust her to dress well enough to mix with his illustrious friends.

'No, I don't, actually.' She dared him to elaborate.

But he seemed to think better of it, saying instead, 'Well, no matter. We don't have to go to that party. Just so long as I see you again.'

If the last held a note of soft urgency, Sara hardly noticed. She was too busy seething at his earlier comments. In fact she might have told him what to do with his party, if he hadn't rung off at that point. Instead she found herself committed to going and, at the same time, obliged to fend off more curious questions from her brother.

Though their conversation had been brief, Dryden's voice had struck a chord with Simon Summerfield, who had once watched the actor in a drama series. The problem was he had a poor memory for names and received no assistance from Sara, despite his mutterings of, 'You know, there's something very familiar about this friend of yours,' and 'Are you sure I couldn't have met him somewhere?'

Sara realised that later he might make the connection,
and, if he did, it was not going to please him one bit.
No way was a womanising actor, however wealthy, going
to be Simon's choice for her.

When he eventually left, still pondering over Neville's
identity, Sara went straight to her wardrobe to debate
the matter of what to wear. She had two choices: either
to dress in a fashion that would embarrass Dryden or
dress so stylishly that it might force him to eat his words.

For the first she'd probably have to go shopping, not
currently owning anything cheap or loud enough. She
pictured herself in gold lamé, fishnet tights and a short
leopardskin coat, and smiled as she imagined Neville
trying to explain her away to his rich, glamorous friends.

Alternatively she could show him she wasn't a complete social disaster. She did have a recent evening gown,
bought for her parents' wedding anniversary party. It
had been a present to her father—her turning up, chic
and stylish, in this beautifully cut dress, when so often
he sighed over her sloppy jerseys and jeans. He'd appreciated it too, proudly declaring her the most beautiful daughter in the world. And, though not vain as a
rule, Sara had also enjoyed looking her best in the dark
red silk.

So those were the choices, and obviously the first must
be favourite, to pay back Neville for his heavy hints on
dress. The only problem was assembling her lurid
costume by this evening. She checked her watch and saw
she had three hours before the shops closed. If she
rushed, she could probably manage it. The question was,
did she have the nerve?

Nerve or not, Sara was ready and waiting when Neville
Dryden arrived a few minutes before nine. She answered
the door in her coat—not the leopardskin one she'd
visualised—but far from glamorous in a waterproof

trenchcoat teamed with woollen neckscarf and plastic rainhat.

For a moment he didn't seem to notice her clothes, slanting her a wide smile of greeting as she opened the door. But the smile slipped when he took in the raincoat, the Paddington hat and the checked muffler, all successfully hiding what she wore beneath. She had to control an impulse to laugh at his expression of dismay.

'Ready?' he finally asked, and to his credit he almost concealed the hope that she might say no, she had yet to dress up.

Instead Sara gave a nod and stepped out, closing the door behind her.

They walked to the car in silence, Neville installing her in the passenger seat before going round to the driver's side. The gesture reminded her of the first time she'd travelled in the Daimler, though that night he'd practically ordered her to get in and had clearly regarded her as a nuisance.

She stole a glance at him—he was clean-shaven once more and looking superb in a dark dinner suit and bowtie. She wondered what he thought of her now. Whatever it might be, she couldn't believe he was interested in her as a person. Surely her life must seem very dull in comparison to his?

Like now, for instance, she felt, as, car in motion, he asked her how she'd spent the last couple of days.

He was obviously just making conversation, but what was she meant to reply? I read a book. I cooked. I did a week's washing. My brother paid me a visit. And so on.

It was hardly riveting stuff, and she couldn't tell him of the hours wasted, planning on how to avoid the exact situation she was now in. So what did she say?

'I didn't do much,' she finally said, shrugging, and turned the conversation back to him. 'What about you?'

He made a slight grimace. 'Well, after getting rid of Superbrat yesterday, I spent the evening attending a charity performance of *Swan Lake*... Do you like ballet, by the way?'

'Not really,' a wary Sara replied.

'Good—because I positively loathe it,' he confided. 'I realise I shouldn't, but personally I find the sight of grown men prancing round a stage in tights more ridiculous than anything else.'

'Actually, so do I,' Sara confessed in return, 'although I'd never dare admit it. Not to my family, anyway. They're all devotees, especially my brother.'

'The one visiting you this afternoon?' Neville asked.

'Yes.'

'Older or younger?'

'Older—a fact I'm not allowed to forget,' she confided drily.

'Bossy, you mean?' Neville concluded.

'That's one word for it.' Sara pulled a face as she recalled her brother's attempts at well-meaning advice. 'Let's just say he always knows best.'

'Or thinks he does?' Neville laughed in sympathy. 'Was he annoyed about your skipping his party? Because we could always go there instead. I'm easy.'

Sara just bet he was. What could have been a generous offer, she read as quite the opposite. Having decided she wasn't dressed to suit his image, he wanted to keep as low a profile as he could.

'Oh, no, your party sounds such a *glamorous* affair,' she said pointedly. 'I'd hate to miss it.'

She was clearly being sarcastic, but his frown suggested he didn't understand why. Perhaps he didn't realise how insulting his less than subtle hints over the telephone had been.

'Well, I warn you now,' he drawled back, 'you may find some of the guests pretty tedious, especially if they start talking theatre.'

'Will it all be actors and actresses?'

'Probably, yes, apart from the occasional playwright, and they can be worse. They get so used to writing everybody's dialogue, they either talk in monologue or don't talk at all.'

Sara laughed, before saying, 'You're very cynical about your friends.'

'You think so?' He lifted a brow at her. 'Then just wait until you've had an evening of their company.'

Sara grimaced. 'You're beginning to make me wish I'd never agreed to go to this party.'

'In that case, we could always go back to my place and have our own private celebration,' he suggested.

'No, thank you,' she said on a prim note, before catching the look that told her he'd been baiting her.

'Somehow I thought you'd say that,' he drawled, soft laughter in his voice. 'In fact, when I called today, I half expected you to chicken out of the party altogether.'

Sara's lips went into an even thinner line. She resented any suggestion she might be scared to go out with him. Sensible wasn't scared.

'There's still time,' she threatened half seriously, but he laughed it off.

'I'm afraid not. We're almost there,' he announced, turning off the main thoroughfare on to a tree-lined avenue.

Sara had been paying little attention to the brief journey. She'd assumed the party would be somewhere around Kensington or Chelsea where he lived, but they had only travelled to neighbouring Wimbledon. It, too, was one of the wealthier boroughs of London, and they slowed before a massive, although fairly modern, house built in Tudor style.

It was fronted by a square forecourt, already packed with cars. Neville still drove the Daimler up to the door, possibly knowing a young man would appear to take responsibility for parking it elsewhere. Sara assumed this service was normal at smart people's parties, and couldn't decide if it was thoughtfulness or just plain ostentation.

'Who's our host, by the way?' she asked as Neville led her inside.

'Hostess,' he corrected. 'Her name's Judith Grant. She's my agent, as well as being a friend.'

'Oh.' Sara memorised the name before they crossed the threshold into a wide, parquet-floored hall. It was teeming with people, the party being the kind that spilled into all available space in the house, and one casual glance round the crowd had her recognising several famous film celebrities—and suddenly wondering what in heaven's name was she doing there.

It wasn't that she was overawed or starstruck. She just hadn't the first idea how to converse with these people. The last film she'd seen was *ET* four years earlier, she couldn't recall the last play, and, as for television, she didn't possess a set. That didn't leave her any common ground at all. Somehow she didn't feel they'd be interested in the daily existence of a social worker.

She noticed herself getting several curious stares and assumed it was through association with Neville. It was only when a maid appeared to take her coat that she remembered her daft plastic hat and woollen neckscarf. She whipped them off quickly, revealing the elegant style in which she'd dressed her hair, drawn back from her face and coiled in a pleated knot at the base of her neck. She then allowed Neville to help her with her trenchcoat, and, sensing some stares lingering, was glad she'd decided on her dark red silk rather than gold lamé.

It was a good choice. Starkly plain in cut, the gown's strapless neckline left bare Sara's fine shoulders and the first rise of her high, full breasts. The bodice was boned to her waist, then it fell to knee-length in a smooth line that made the silk cling to her hips as she moved.

Yet it wasn't the dress that held men's attention. It was the effect—the translucence of bare skin, the subtle sway of hips and rustle of silk, the sheer understated sensuality of it all.

The effect was even more potent in Neville's case, unexpected as it was. Based on the coat and hat, he'd prepared himself for a dowdily plain or unfashionably odd dress. When he saw how wrong he'd been, he was too stunned to hide his reaction.

At first Sara felt satisfaction, knowing her sophistication had come as a surprise. Then he continued to stare at her, with a look that went past flattery and compliments, and conveyed exactly what he was thinking—exactly what he was imagining as his gaze travelled downwards.

The look was so explicit that Sara forgot they were in a room full of people, and only saw it, too—Neville undressing her just as his eyes were doing, his hands smoothing over the silk in the same slow, intent way. The breath caught in her throat and she tried to pretend the idea offended her. She told herself it did, even though her body trembled, saying something altogether different.

And when his eyes returned to her face something he saw there made him smile—a smile that suggested that, if she was fooling anyone, it certainly wasn't him.

'You're beautiful,' he said quite simply, as if he'd just discovered the fact.

Sara did not reply, sure her voice would betray her.

Then, as they continued to stare at each other, a voice intruded, calling over the crowd, 'Neville. Neville, darling!'

Finally tearing her eyes from his, Sara looked round in time to see a voluptuous redhead approaching them. Dressed in a gown of silver satin, she gave full meaning to the word flamboyant as she arrived to fling her arms round Neville and press a lingering kiss on his mouth.

Forced to take a step backwards, Sara was left feeling very much like a spare part. For, if Neville hadn't initiated the embrace, he certainly didn't seem to be struggling too hard to escape it.

When the redhead finally came up for air, it was to repeat in a purr, 'Neville, darling.'

Sara wondered if this was a sign of a very limited vocabulary.

There was certainly a hint of mockery in the way Neville returned the greeting, 'Diana, *darling*.'

Diana darling didn't seem to notice as she went on to demand, 'What are you doing here? I thought you were spending New Year with your appalling mother.'

'I was,' Neville confirmed, 'but, as you see, I had a slight change of plans.'

In saying this, he stretched out a hand to catch Sara's and pull her back to his side. The gesture implied, quite falsely, that she was the main reason for his change of plans.

Plainly the other woman read it that way as she included Sara in the conversation by sliding her a less than delighted glance.

Neville went on to introduce them. 'Diana, I'd like you to meet Sara Peters. Sara, this is Diana Redmond, an actress of some small repute.'

'Small repute!' Diana gasped at this gross understatement, before demanding of Sara, 'I mean, how many actresses can fill a West End theatre on their name alone?'

Sara decided on a diplomatic, if lukewarm, reply of, 'Not many, I should imagine.'

But Neville put in drily, 'At least Diana assumes it's her name, not that of her rather famous male co-star.'

'That has-been!' Diana wrinkled her nose in disgust. 'He's so wooden they could have used him for the scenery. He's only lucky he's playing a drunk so he can act in character.'

Neville laughed shortly. 'Would that be the same actor you called "a man of infinitely versatile talent"?'

'That was to the papers, darling.' Diana Redmond pouted, then turned back to Sara. 'So what are *you* in?'

'Social work,' Sara replied briefly.

'Social Work?' the other woman echoed as if she'd never heard of such a thing. 'It sounds like one of those dreary, depressing, true-life dramas. Where's it playing?'

'Fulham, mainly,' Sara couldn't resist saying, although she realised they had their wires crossed. It seemed to amuse Neville as he sent her a smile over the actress's head.

Diana Redmond replied with a scornful, 'Fulham? God, I didn't even know there was a theatre there. Still, I suppose it's marginally better than playing somewhere in the sticks.'

'Like Scarborough, for instance?' Neville suggested, and received a glare for his trouble. It didn't stop him from revealing, 'That's where Diana first started in pantomime—playing Dick Whittington's cat.'

It was obvious he was joking, at least about the 'cat' part, but the actress still protested, 'I did nothing of the kind! I was the lead in *Cinderella*, if you must know... *And* it was Great Yarmouth.'

'I stand corrected,' Neville said, with a smile that was hardly repentant.

Sara was also having difficulty hiding amusement, and it was to her Diana Redmond directed her cattiness.

'I was only seventeen at the time,' the actress declared, before continuing pointedly, 'At that age, you're glad of anything, but personally *I* couldn't bear to be thirty and *still* struggling. All credit to you, though, dear.'

The 'dear' was about as phoney as the actress's smile, and Sara was torn between laughing the whole thing off or simply walking away from this dreadful woman.

Neville got in first, finally admitting, 'Actually, you misunderstood. Sara is literally a social worker.'

'In real life, you mean?' Diana Redmond's eyes widened with simulated horror. 'My God, that sounds even drearier. Still, I suppose you get a kick out of do-gooding,' she dismissed airily.

And Sara found herself counting to ten again, before agreeing, 'Occasionally, but you learn to take evasive action.'

Neville understood immediately and laughed in appreciation. Diana, however, demanded, 'Is that some kind of joke?'

Sara shrugged, leaving the woman to take it how she wanted.

'More a comment on our times, I'd say,' Neville volunteered in an amused drawl, and, while the actress was still trying to catch up, brought the conversation to an end with, 'However, we mustn't bore you with real life, darling.'

He gave Diana Redmond a last sardonic smile and left her staring daggers after them, as he steered Sara through the hall to an equally crowded drawing-room.

'Sorry about that,' he murmured in apology, 'but what Diana lacks in brain-power, she tends to make up for in bitchiness.'

'So I noticed.' Sara grimaced, wondering if all his female friends were in the same mould.

Neville seemed to read her thoughts, as he went on, 'Come and meet our hostess. I'm sure you'll find her a distinct improvement.'

He took Sara's hand, as if it were the most natural action in the world, and led the way towards a group of people standing at the fireplace. The central figure was a middle-aged woman, with greying hair and a lined face, made attractive by the intelligence behind it. She wore a smart rather than glamorous dress in green linen, and held court by the sheer force of her personality.

When she spotted the couple approaching, she immediately excused herself from the conversation to greet them. She offered a bony cheek for Neville to kiss, and, unlike Diana Redmond, acknowledged Sara without delay.

'Well, aren't you going to introduce us?' she demanded of Neville, before he really had the chance to do so.

'If I must,' he said and laughed at her bullying tone, then went on, 'Sara, this crusty old broad is Judith Grant—my Mr Ten-per-cent, one might say. Judith, this is Sara Peters...a friend of mine.'

At this tongue-in-cheek introduction, Judith Grant snorted, 'Old, indeed!'

While Sara murmured a polite, 'Pleased to meet you.'

'Likewise, I'm sure,' Judith Grant said in an accent that betrayed her American origins. 'You know I've already heard a great deal about you, Mrs Peters.'

'You have?' Sara directed a quick, accusing glance at Neville.

But he held up his hands, protesting, 'Don't look at me! Superbrat's the one she's been grilling.'

Judith Grant did not deny it, saying instead to Sara, 'I really don't know how he has the nerve to call Scott that, when you consider what an absolute monster *he* was as a boy. I remember the first time I met him. He was ten and I was...let's just say, the right side of thirty. Anyway, he had to be the nastiest, rudest——'

'Yes, well,' Neville interrupted smartly, 'I'm sure Sara can't be in the least interested in my childhood.'

'Aren't you?' the older woman asked, a decided twinkle in her eyes.

Sara played up by assuring, 'On the contrary, I'm fascinated.'

'See?' Judith Grant gave Neville a triumphant look, then suggested, 'So while we girls have a chat, why don't you fetch us a drink?'

Neville didn't seem too happy at the idea, but he asked both their choice, and, with a half-pleading, half-warning glance at their hostess, reluctantly departed for the bar in the adjoining lounge.

Watching him disappear in the crowd, Judith Grant went on, 'I wasn't kidding, you know. He sure was a little monster.'

'I can believe it,' Sara remarked drily.

The American woman chuckled, before adding in a more serious vein, 'Not that you could blame him, poor kid! With David and Felice as parents, anyone would be mixed-up. Has he told you about them?'

Sara shook her head. 'Not really.'

'You'll know they were both film stars, of course,' Judith Grant assumed. 'In fact, I was his father's agent for years, before I married and came to live in London. A charming man, David, but irresponsible as hell and a complete fool where women were concerned. Every second film, he'd fall in love with his female co-star, then spend months agonising over how to ask Felice for a divorce.'

Sara frowned. 'But they stayed married, didn't they?'

'For better or worse,' Judith Grant confirmed, 'and mostly it was worse. Felice was hardly a saint herself, affairs-wise, but mention divorce and all of a sudden she'd remember what a good Catholic girl she was. Either that or she'd threaten him with a fight over Neville's custody.'

'I thought Neville lived with his grandfather in London,' Sara recalled.

The American woman nodded. 'Yes, but that was the point. You see, David wasn't much of a father, but at least he recognised the fact, and knew Neville was better off away from the influence of Hollywood and Felice. That's why the threat worked. She didn't want the boy— never had—but she'd have taken him out of spite.'

'Did he realise how his mother felt?' Sara asked.

'I'd say so,' Judith replied. 'He'd lost most of his illusions by the time I met him. It was at LA Airport, I remember. He'd come over for a vacation, and I was collecting him as a favour to David who was busy filming. Felice was off, God knows where. Just ten, the kid was, but he'd already perfected that superior look of his... You know the one?'

'Oh, *yes*,' Sara agreed with emphasis, and the other woman laughed.

'Anyway, he looked me up and down, then asked me if I was the new chauffeur or just his father's latest tart!'

'My God! What did you do?'

'Nothing. I was too stunned. I mean, I'd been expecting a polite English schoolboy, not some hoodlum.'

'Was he any better with his parents?'

The older woman grimaced. 'Not significantly, but then they didn't take much notice. Maybe that was the point—he was trying to get their attention.'

'That's possible.' In Sara's experience, bad behaviour was often a form of attention-seeking.

'Or maybe he just wanted to make sure they sent him back to his grandfather's,' Judith continued. 'Whichever, it was some time before I realised that, underneath the hoodlum, there was a rather special little kid.'

She smiled reminiscently while Sara murmured a polite, 'Really,' and masked her sense of disbelief.

Judith detected it all the same. 'Oh, I know it might be difficult to credit. Even now, he can be an awkward cuss if he chooses. But there's a fine streak in him, too, when things really matter. Take the way he's looked after Scott.'

'Yes, well...' Sara was unable to see anything exceptional in this. To her mind, it was the least any decent father would do.

But Judith obviously viewed it differently. 'I mean, if you consider the way Annie let him down—not to mention his own father—it's a wonder he has any time for Scott... You do know about Annie, don't you?'

Sara nodded. 'I understand they met at drama school.'

'Yes, that's so. I don't know how serious they were,' Judith went on, 'but I think he was pretty cut up when she dumped him.'

Sara's eyes widened in shocked surprise. From the start, she'd assumed Neville had done the dumping. But he'd never actually said so, had he? Now she was left wondering if his experience with Annie had made him ruthless with other women.

'Did she realise she was pregnant?' she asked.

'Oh, yes, she was quite open about it,' Judith Grant declared. 'And, naturally, the pregnancy made it harder for Neville to accept the situation. Maybe he did love her, I don't know. She was a very pretty girl, I remember, but not a strong character... You don't mind my talking about all this, do you?' she added, as she sensed Sara's uneasiness.

'Not as such,' Sara replied, 'but I'm not sure if Neville would appreciate it.'

'I'm positive he wouldn't,' Judith stated unrepentantly. '*That's* not going to stop me, though, because I think it's important you appreciate how much of Neville's behaviour is sheer defensiveness. You do see that, don't you?'

'Yes, well...' Again Sara was more polite than convinced. She might have a new perspective on his relationship with Scott's mother, but she still believed a good part of Neville Dryden's behaviour could be put down to sheer bloody-mindedness.

'He won't thank me for interfering, I know that,' Judith ran on, 'and normally I wouldn't bother. The majority of his women are conceited little bimbos, who are after what they can get and deserve to be treated accordingly. But he's made it clear you're different, so——'

'Look, Mrs Grant,' Sara decided it was time to interrupt, 'I don't know what Neville's told you, but——'

'Oh, don't worry!' Judith overruled her with a dry chuckle. 'He was remarkably honest, I imagine. He told me, and I quote, "She's too smart to be taken in by my charm, and too tough to want to be." May I ask if he's right?'

'More or less,' Sara said, but on a defensive note, for he'd made her sound rather hard.

'Yet you went out with him tonight,' the other woman added, a speculative look in her eye.

'He didn't give me much choice,' Sara recalled.

'No, he can be quite overpowering.' A smile crossed the American's face, suggesting she regarded it as a positive quality.

To Sara's mind, the word 'overpowering' could also apply to Judith Grant. Why else was she, Sara, allowing herself to be drawn into a personal conversation with a virtual stranger—particularly when the subject was Neville Dryden?

'But I believe he's worth the effort,' the other continued earnestly. 'Just give him a chance, honey.'

'A chance to do what?' was asked, not by Sara, but Neville, who'd returned, unobserved, with the drinks.

Judith Grant didn't seem in the least disconcerted as she answered bluntly, 'To show her that, underneath it all, you're a really nice guy.'

'Good lord, Judith!' He pulled a face at her choice of words. 'What are you trying to do—ruin my reputation? A "nice guy"? It sounds like something one should burn on November the fifth.'

'OK, smarty, I don't know why I'm wasting my breath.' Judith shook her head in defeat, and, taking the champagne glass he held out, departed with a last, 'The girl's probably too good for you, anyway.'

Neville just laughed at the comment, before turning back to Sara. 'With friends like Judy, who needs enemies? I take it she told you what a thoroughly obnoxious child I was.'

'She seemed to think you had reason to be,' Sara replied.

'Perhaps.' He dismissed the subject with a shrug, just as a couple came to join them.

Neville introduced her to the newcomers, a TV producer and his wife, and soon Sara was chatting quite easily with the other woman. She was an ex-actress who appeared to have no regrets about giving up a moderately successful career to bring up her family. Unlike Diana Redmond, she showed an intelligent interest in Sara's work, and the conversation gradually moved on to a general discussion on modern-day social problems.

More people joined their group, but Sara remained relaxed, discovering that, by and large, Neville's friends were easy to talk to. A few were as self-absorbed as he'd warned, but they required little conversational effort, apart from a nod in the right place. Most Sara found to have a wide variety of interests outside the film and theatre world, and a lively if sometimes caustic sense of humour.

Naturally some were rather curious about her relationship with Neville, but, when asked how they'd met, she avoided the truth with a vague 'through mutual friends'. It seemed wiser than saying they'd first ran into each other at Fulham Police Station, and Neville awarded her an approving glance at her less controversial explanation.

As the evening progressed, Sara also became aware of how well-regarded Neville was among his contemporaries. At first, she thought it was simply his wry charm which attracted people, but then she noticed how often his opinion was sought. It surprised her, too, that, where some womanisers were disliked by their own sex, Neville appeared popular with both. Perhaps this was because he stuck to his rule never to become involved with married or attached women, so his male friends did not have to worry what effect his charm might be having on their partners.

That it did have an effect, Sara could not deny. She felt it herself, every time she looked up and their eyes met and he smiled at her in a way that excluded the rest of the world. She felt herself slipping under the spell, wanting to believe she really was special to him.

But common sense still prevailed. She knew that, if she'd caught Neville's attention for now, she would not hold it for long. It wasn't modesty that told her this, just recognising the kind of man he was.

At one time there might have been a chance for him to be different. Long ago, perhaps, before his parents had made life and love seem like a battleground, or before Annie had confirmed that impression. But now it was many years too late, and life and love had become a game to him, a game in which he would never be the loser. That part was cast for her or any other woman foolish enough to play along. And *she* wasn't going to be that foolish... was she?

CHAPTER EIGHT

LATER in the evening, Neville led Sara through to the living-room where couples were dancing. The lights had been dimmed to create an intimate atmosphere but, before they could take to the floor, an attractive blonde descended on them. She announced to Sara that her name was Barbara and it had been simply an age since she'd last seen Neville, so he simply had to come and dance with her. He was given little chance to excuse himself as the blonde dragged him away.

Sara gravitated towards a corner, and wasn't there long before a tall, slim girl appeared at her side.

'So *you* were the one,' the girl said without any preamble.

Sara returned her stare with a vague sense of recognition. 'Sorry, have we met?'

'Come on, don't play the innocent,' the girl retorted. 'I'm Jane Baxter—the girl he dumped for you. Remember?'

Sara frowned for another second or two, then it hit her—Janey, the girl who'd been with Neville the night they'd met.

'Yes, of course.' She made an effort to be polite. 'How are you?'

'Fat lot you care,' the girl threw back. 'If you did, you wouldn't go around nicking other people's fellas. Still, you'll know how it feels soon enough.'

She nodded towards Neville, dancing with the blonde who currently claimed his attention.

'Now, look here, I did not——' Sara began to protest.

'Save it!' Janey cut in. 'I don't need your apologies. Just remember I'll be laughing when he dumps you, too,' she jeered, and, with a last sour look, stomped off.

Sara, who had not been about to apologise, was left gritting her teeth. She was still gritting them when Neville returned, minus his dancing partner.

'Was that Janey?' he asked with stunning nonchalance.

'It certainly was,' Sara ground back.

He picked up her annoyance, and added, 'What was she saying to you?'

'What do you think?' she countered, sure he must know the gist.

If he did, his shrug dismissed Janey as unimportant, and, taking Sara's hand, he led her on to the dance floor.

Sara, however, was still smarting at Janey's accusations, and she stiffened as he tried to draw her into his arms.

'Not good, at any rate,' he said in an amused undertone.

'What?' Sara snapped in reply.

'Well, either I have the sort of problem only my best friend will tell me about,' he drawled, 'or the lovely Janey has told you I'm bad news.'

'I hardly need someone of Janey's intellect to point *that* out,' Sara threw back.

'No, I suppose not,' he agreed with the same irritating good humour.

It prompted Sara to continue, 'However, as you brought it up, she warned me you have a rapid turnover in female companions.'

'I see.' His smile thinned a little. 'Well, it's lucky for me you're a more discerning type of woman—the type that doesn't automatically believe everything she hears.'

'I——' Sara was stuck for an appropriate reply, which was of course his intention. If she said she did believe

Janey, that would bring her down to the other girl's level. If she said she didn't, she would be lying.

While she searched for a suitable response, Neville took advantage of her distraction to pull her closer until he was almost holding her.

Sara would have to struggle to free herself and she was loath to do so. She didn't want *him* thinking she was affected by his nearness.

It was hard enough convincing *herself* she wasn't. She tried distancing her thoughts from him, but he made it impossible. When he smoothed his hand over her back and touched the warmth of her bare skin, the breath caught in her throat. Then his other hand enclosed hers and pressed it to his body so she could feel the strong beat of his heart. His cheek was resting against her hair and, while they barely swayed to the music, he slowly trailed his lips to the pulse at her temple. She felt her whole body begin to tremble, to betray her, yet still she didn't pull away. Instead, she let herself dream a little, pretending it was for real, the loving way he held her, the confusion of tenderness and passion she felt in return.

Dance merged into dance as they circled the dimly lit room, lost in each other, all but making love with the touch of their hands and the sway of their bodies. Until it no longer seemed like craziness—she and Neville. It no longer seemed to matter who he was or how many women there had been. All that mattered was the way he made her feel.

Then the music suddenly stopped and the lights were raised, and mercifully sanity returned. Without their noticing, midnight had approached and the other guests were preparing to usher in the New Year.

Sara started to pull away from him and he cursed softly but let her go. They were carried by the drift of the crowd to the hallway, where a grandfather clock had been placed so the hour could be counted down.

It was done so, by various voices more or less in unison, then at the stroke of twelve a general shout of 'Happy New Year' was given out, and, amid the blowing of hooters and paper trumpets, the usual kisses and handshakes and back-thumps were exchanged.

Sara turned to Neville, and, echoing another 'Happy New Year', offered her hand to him.

But the gesture was ignored, as she'd half known it would be. Instead he lifted his own hand to cup her cheek, and, at the gentle caress of his fingers, she closed her eyes, accepting the inevitable. She felt the cool whisper of his breath on her face as, regardless of the jostling, cheering crowd around them, he lowered his mouth to cover hers. Then the noise seemed to fade and the people disappear and there was just his kiss, breathless, endless, consuming, as the attraction between them, subtle and unspoken, flared into a desire too blatant to need words.

Over and over they kissed, his mouth warm and hard on hers, parting her lips, invading her senses, until her only thought was of him, her only emotion for him. This time there was no ghost between them, no doubts, nothing but a passion going wildly out of control.

It was the crowd that brought them back again, clapping and jeering, reminding them they weren't alone. When Neville finally raised his head, it was to find they had an audience vicariously enjoying their kiss.

Colour flooded Sara's cheeks at the laughter and ribald remarks which greeted them, and she sank into the background, as friends and acquaintances gathered round to wish him 'Happy New Year'.

She might have slunk away altogether if she'd been sure of escaping without an argument. Instead she watched with an impassive face as a succession of pretty women presented themselves for a kiss. She felt no jealousy, just a sobering awareness that there had been a long line of women before her—and there would be a long line after.

'Are you OK?' he asked when he eventually returned to catch her serious expression.

'Yes, fine,' she said quickly, not about to reveal her thoughts.

'But you've had enough?' he suggested, scanning the crowd that had become considerably rowdier since midnight had struck.

Sara shrugged, leaving the decision to him, and he went on, 'Well, I wouldn't mind leaving. If you fetch your coat, I'll relay our thanks to Judith.'

'All right.' Sara nodded, and went in search of the maid who'd hung up the coats in a long corridor off the main hall. It didn't take long to locate hers—being the only trenchcoat and silly hat handed over.

She met up with Neville in the outer hall, and they waited for his car to be brought to the front drive. Silence reigned as they climbed into the Daimler and drove off. It seemed a heavy silence after the noise of the party.

It was Neville who finally broke it, by asking quietly, 'Will you come home with me?'

Sara was taken by surprise. Kensington was miles away. 'For a drink, you mean?' she said uncertainly.

'No, to spend the night with me,' he replied, again in a quiet voice, but this time making his meaning very clear.

'I——' Sara was more confused than angry. She hadn't expected him to be so direct.

'I'd like you to... very much,' he added in a persuasive tone, yet still unlike the approach she'd expected, the seductive ploys she'd imagined him using.

'I... No, thank you,' she eventually said, the politeness sounding absurd in the circumstances.

She waited for the pressure, the claim that she wanted him—a fact so obvious in the way she'd responded to his kiss. She steeled herself for his derision when she tried to explain that wanting wasn't enough for her, that there had to be love.

She waited in vain. For a moment he seemed ready to argue the matter, then he simply shrugged.

Sara felt she had just been put in her place—attractive enough to take to bed, but not attractive enough to fight for. It was a salutary lesson.

That he wasn't greatly affected became plain as he turned the conversation to small talk, asking her opinion of various people she'd met. She followed his lead, determined to show she wasn't affected either. Why should she be? He'd asked, she'd refused, end of story.

At least she thought so, until they reached her house and he insisted on seeing her to the door, even though he'd parked by her gate.

She seemed to be all fingers and thumbs as she tried to unlock the front door, and perhaps he genuinely wished to help as he took the key from her hand and fitted it into the Yale lock.

Then, as they stood facing each other in the porchway, he said, 'The answer's—yes, please.'

'What?' Sara didn't know the question.

'Would I like to be your first foot and come in for a drink?' he supplied.

Reluctant to invite him inside, Sara searched for an excuse. 'I only have wine in the house.'

'Wine would be fine,' he smiled back.

'It's home-made nettle,' she threatened.

'Good,' he countered, and, before she could make up a new excuse—or even tell him the truth—he stepped over the threshold.

A resigned Sara showed him the way into her flat. She had no fear he would force himself on her. What concerned her was how thin her own resistance seemed to be wearing.

'I appear to have some whisky, too,' she admitted after a quick search of her modest drink supply.

'Please,' he accepted the offer. 'Make it a small measure, though. I don't want to be over the limit.'

'All right,' Sara agreed, surprised by his moderation. She'd imagined show-business types always drank like fish but, thinking back on it, he had drunk little that evening. 'Is that OK?'

'Fine,' he said at the glass she held out. 'Could I possibly have something in it?'

'Water?' she offered the only option, conscious of being a rather poor hostess.

'That'll do.' He smiled a little.

With no answering smile, she invited him to take a seat, before she went through to the kitchen for the water. She returned to find him still standing, although he'd moved to the fireplace. His back was to her but she knew he was studying her wedding photograph on the mantelpiece. She prepared herself for some curious or crass comment, but none was forthcoming.

All he said was, 'You were young, weren't you?'

'Twenty-one,' she admitted, a shade defensively.

'You look younger,' he remarked on her open, radiant face in the picture, then dropped the subject as she handed him his drink and he chinked their glasses together. 'Well, Happy New Year.'

'Yes . . . Happy New Year,' she echoed, but nervously, as she waited for him to make some kind of move.

He did so suddenly. A very simple move as he drained his glass and leaned forward to lightly kiss her cheek.

'Look after yourself, Sara Peters,' he said with apparent sincerity, then, with a last, regretful smile, walked out of the flat. And the house. And, she realised, her life.

She listened to his car start up and drive away, and she began to feel a curious sense of loss, then the dull pain of loneliness.

She picked up the wedding photograph as if to remind herself what love was about—two people committing themselves for a lifetime. But it suddenly seemed so long ago, that day she'd been a bride. And her love for Nick was gradually becoming just memories that would fade with time.

The truth was Neville Dryden was more real to her now. Not that she loved him—she couldn't love a man like that. Not that she was even sure she liked him. But oh, she could want him, want him so badly it scared her.

And, in the end, it was no comfort that she'd done the right thing. No comfort at all.

CHAPTER NINE

SARA fell back into her normal routine: work early, home late, a good book, then bed. But she had changed. For no longer could she hide from the emptiness of her life, and what little satisfaction she'd drawn from her job seemed to have gone, too.

'I think I've just ceased caring,' was how she expressed it to Bob, when the couple invited her upstairs for tea one cold February evening.

'Not you,' Bob protested. 'Your dedication makes the rest of us look like charity workers. Take that Simpson kid—the things you did for him.'

Sara pulled a face. 'Good try, Bob—bad example. Dear little Darren's just graduated from youth custody to Wandsworth.'

'Oh.' Bob looked as if he'd like to kick himself. 'Yes, well . . . that doesn't mean you don't care. You tried hard enough, you just can't win them all.'

'No, but it would be nice to win one or two,' she said with a sigh.

'Come on, you've had a good few successes,' he pointed out.

'Have I?' Sara's tone cast doubt on it. 'Sometimes I think the kids that go straight would do anyway, without my interference.'

'Yes, I've had that thought myself,' Bob confided, this time expressing some of his own disillusionment. It was hard to keep optimistic in their job. 'Well, if you're considering jacking it in, I wouldn't altogether blame you,' he added kindly.

But Sara shook her head, knowing she'd blame herself. Someone had to keep trying. 'What else would I do?' she said and shrugged.

'Lots of things,' his wife Kathy inserted. 'Teach, write a book, sail round the world.'

'In which order?' Sara smiled at these ambitious suggestions, then dismissed her troubles, saying, 'Oh, never mind me. I'm just having a moan. Post-Christmas blues, I expect.'

'I know the feeling,' Bob groaned in sympathy, and went on to complain about his own work problems.

It was later, when he'd disappeared to watch TV, that Kathy said, 'I hope you don't mind my asking, but is it just work that's getting you down?'

'What else?' Sara gave another shrug.

But if she expected Kathy to be too tactful to pursue it, she was mistaken. 'I wondered if you were having problems with your actor friend.'

'No,' Sara replied simply, without any attempt to provide explanations.

Kathy still wasn't discouraged. 'May I ask what happened? I mean, you don't have to tell me if you don't want to.'

'You'll just never offer me dinner again?' Sara joked, aware her friend was almost bursting with curiosity.

'No, of course not.' Kathy sounded a little offended. 'I may regard you as a friend rather than our landlady, but either way I respect your right to privacy.'

'Thank you,' Sara replied with suitable gravity, then waited.

It wasn't long before the younger girl prompted. 'Well?'

'He asked me to sleep with him, I politely declined, and we called it quits,' Sara relayed flatly.

'What?' Her frankness made Kathy gasp.

'He asked me to sleep with him, I pol——'

'Yes, all right, I did understand, Sara. I just can't believe it was that simple.'

'Oh, it was,' Sara confirmed, this time a trace of bitterness in her voice.

Kathy picked it up as she replied, 'I'm sorry, love.'

'Don't be.' Sara shook her head, conveying how impossible the whole thing had been. After all, what had she and Neville Dryden had in common? Nothing.

Yet he still dominated her thoughts, that night as most others. They'd met only four times, the last over a month ago, but he'd left his mark all the same. In his careless, arrogant, selfish way, he'd wandered into her life, casually turned it upside-down, and just as casually wandered out again. By now, he probably couldn't even remember her name.

But she remembered. Everything about him she remembered—the drawl in his voice and that lazy smile and those dark blue bedroom eyes. She remembered how he'd made her feel—so angry, at times, but so alive, too. And, when the arguments had become another kind of passion, he'd made her senses reel with the simple touch of a hand.

If she'd turned him down, it hadn't been for any moral reason. She just couldn't have stood the humiliation of being discarded like all the women before her. And might there not have been a little pain, too? She didn't need that; she'd already had enough pain for a lifetime when she'd lost Nick. So, yes, she'd done the right thing.

It was only late at night, lying sleepless, that her certainty wavered. Then it seemed the cowardly thing. Living a nice, boring, painless existence. Not really living at all—just going through the motions.

But what should she have done? she asked herself. Gone to bed with Neville and risked all that pain and humiliation? She shook her head at this absurdity, and once more told herself to forget the man.

*   *   *

She tried hard to, in the following week, busying herself with work, shutting out dangerous thoughts. She felt she was succeeding, too, until the Friday afternoon when she was leaving the office with a couple of friends, and there he was—large as life, at the foot of the steps, leaning negligently against his Daimler, which was parked just as negligently on a double yellow line.

For a second Sara just froze and stared at him, her heart beating like a drum as a familiar smile spread over his handsome face. Then she tore her eyes away, and, in near panic, walked on with her friends. But if she thought such an obvious snub would put him off, she was quite wrong.

'Sara!' he shouted after her. 'Wait up, would you?'

It was her companions who stopped and glanced round. Looks of enquiry quickly gave way to stunned recognition. It seemed Sara was the only person ignorant of his fame.

Always in command of a situation, he ran on, 'Didn't you see me, darling? You really must have those lenses checked, you know.'

'I——' Sara opened her mouth and just as hastily shut it. After all, what could she say? He knew perfectly well she'd seen him. He also must know the effect his 'darling' would have, as her friends became even more round-eyed.

'Well, aren't you going to introduce me to these charming ladies?' he prompted.

With little choice to do otherwise, she introduced the women, 'Joyce Millar, Sandy Cooper,' then mumbled his name, 'Neville Dryden.'

There was a small silence, before the older woman, Joyce, had sufficient aplomb to say, 'Nice to meet you, Mr Dryden.'

'And you,' he echoed, offering his broadest smile to both Sara's friends.

It seemed to reduce Sandy, a very junior typist, to a state of dumb awe, and she simply stared at him with a look that set Sara's teeth on edge.

'I thought I'd come and collect you from the office,' Neville continued, making it sound an everyday occurrence. 'May I also offer these ladies a lift?'

'A lift?' Sandy gulped as if he'd offered her a trip to the Bahamas.

But she wasn't given the chance to accept, as Joyce spoke for both of them, saying, 'Thanks very much but we have shopping to do,' before smiling at Sara, saying, 'See you Monday,' and almost dragging an open-mouthed Sandy away.

The moment they were alone, Sara rounded on the actor. 'What the hell are you doing?'

'Doing?' he repeated in a bland tone. 'As I said, collecting you from work.'

'That's not what I meant!' Sara hissed. 'You turn up, out of the blue, and at my office of all places, then make it worse by calling attention to yourself. I have to work with those people, you know.'

'So?' He shrugged. 'I wasn't rude to them, was I?'

'No, but...'

'But what?'

'I...' Unable to explain, Sara threw him an exasperated glance.

He caught on. 'You're worried I might ruin your reputation. Is that it?' he said in amused tones.

'Well, if you must know,' Sara retorted, 'yes, I am. I mean, what must they think, with you throwing *darlings* all over the place.'

'One darling, that was all,' Neville pointed out, 'and they probably think I'm fond of you. Which, of course, I am...at least, sometimes, though not quite at present.'

'Very funny!' Sara gave him a sour look for making a joke out of what she considered a serious matter. 'More likely they think we're...we're intimate.' She chose the least explicit word she could find.

Neville didn't share her reticence. 'You mean they'll think we're sleeping together, just because I called you darling? Heavens, what dirty minds your friends must have.'

'They do not!' Sara snapped back, and wished she'd never started this. 'It's just...well, they both recognised you and they've probably read gossip about your private life. So they're bound to conclude that you and I...that we...' She searched for another clinical way of expressing it but, at the smile lifting the corners of his mouth, she gave up, muttering instead, 'Oh, to hell with it!'

She would have walked away, but he caught her arm. 'All right, I take the point, and, if you want, I'll fix things.'

'How?' She scowled back.

'I don't know. Perhaps I could catch up with your friends and tell them,' he offered.

'Tell them what?' she demanded.

He shrugged, then suggested, 'That I'm *not* sleeping with you, I suppose.'

It was, of course, a ridiculous idea, and by the half-amused look on his face, he knew it.

So did Sara, realising also that she'd over-reacted to the whole situation. It was hardly the end of the world, even if the women had jumped to the wrong conclusions. In fact, she'd probably gone up miles in Sandy's estimation, considering the soppy way the girl had looked at him.

'Forget it!' She dismissed the subject, and tried to shrug off his detaining hand.

He held on, saying, 'OK, let's start again. May I drive you home, Mrs Peters?'

His politeness had little effect on Sara, who saw mockery behind it. She replied flatly, 'No, you may not.'

'Why?' he asked immediately, and it brought back echoes of other arguments.

'Besides the obvious reasons,' she responded, 'I'm not going home. I have a last call to make.'

'Work, you mean?'

'Yes, and I'm already running late.'

As soon as she said it, Sara recognised her mistake. By then, it was too late, as he jumped in, 'So you definitely need a lift.'

He steered her back to the car before she could find a new excuse, and deposited her in the passenger seat. Then he quickly rounded to the driver's side, giving her little time to consider an escape bid.

'Where to?' he asked when they'd pulled away from the kerb.

'Wandsworth.'

'That's a big area. Where exactly?'

'The Hightrees Estate, but you can drop me off on the main road.'

'Don't be silly. It's as easy to take you to the door. Just give me directions.'

'OK.' Sara shrugged. 'I imagine your car's insured.'

'What?' He looked confused at this apparent *non sequitur*, but Sara didn't bother enlightening him.

Instead she said, 'Have you a cigarette?' She hadn't smoked since Christmas but suddenly she felt the need for one.

''Fraid not. I promised Scott I'd puff my last on New Year's Eve,' he relayed, 'and, despite various... frustrations, let's say... I've stuck to it.'

A glance suggested she was included in these frustrations, but Sara ignored it, and decided to keep quiet about her own kicking of the habit.

She confined herself to giving rather brusque directions while she silently wondered why he'd reappeared in her life. He certainly made no attempt to tell her.

It took almost half an hour to reach the estate. Despite its name, there were no trees, high or otherwise, just a concrete maze of flats, with scruffily dressed kids lurking at corners and cars looking as if they'd got caught in a war zone.

They drew to a halt some yards from a group of boys throwing stones at a street lamp. 'If you drive off quickly, they shouldn't attack,' she advised, only half joking.

'Don't be ridiculous. I'm coming with you.' He climbed out of the car before she could stop him.

But, when he arrived at her side, she said, 'Listen, I'm not kidding. It's not a good idea to leave a car here, especially a posh one.'

'All right, hold on,' he instructed, and, much to Sara's consternation, strolled over to the youths. She couldn't hear what he was saying, but she saw him hand one of the boys something.

'What did you give him?' she asked when he returned.

'A complimentary ticket to my next play,' he said, straight-faced. 'It seems he's a theatre-lover.'

For a moment Sara took him seriously, her amazed look saying as much, then its absurdity struck her, and she changed to scowling.

'Actually, I gave him one half of a twenty-pound note, the other half to be handed over if my car's still intact on our return,' he relayed in a smug tone.

'How clever,' Sara said. She supposed he'd picked up that sort of stunt working in films.

'Thanks,' he replied, still looking pleased with himself as he took her arm and began walking towards the nearest entrance.

Sara felt obliged to point out, 'It's a pity your car stereo's worth more. And your tyres, I should imagine. Not to mention, of course, the sheer mind-blowing pleasure of scratching all that nice, shiny black paintwork.'

'What a cynic you are, Mrs Peters,' he said and tutted in response. 'Don't you think we should have a little faith? Maybe that's what these kids need, a little faith coupled with some responsibility.'

'Really?' Sara's lips tightened at this lecture. It was not so different from the line she used to take; she just didn't appreciate having it preached back at her.

She forged ahead of him through the double doors to the lift which was, remarkably, working. As they climbed to the fourth floor, she remained silent while he read, with great fascination, some of the graffiti on the walls. Then they walked out along an open balcony, Sara counting down the flat numbers. Some were boarded up, unoccupied. Others had their front doors reinforced with bars. The estate suffered one of the worst crime rates in London.

'You stay here,' she instructed as they stopped by a pillar. 'I should be about a quarter of an hour. If I'm longer, go without me.'

'And let you wander round this warren on your own?' He was clearly appalled by the idea.

Sara sighed loudly. 'What do you think I normally do? Hire Securicor?'

'I don't know.' Neville realised there were angles about her work he hadn't considered, and, now he did, he didn't like them. 'You should at least go round in pairs.'

'We try to, but the department's overstretched,' she explained briefly. 'Anyway, if you want to wait, that's up to you. Just don't interfere, no matter what happens.'

'Why? What's likely to happen?' he demanded, no longer finding any humour in the situation.

'Nothing, probably,' Sara dismissed, and walked off before he could press her.

She realised now how foolish it had been letting him accompany her. Not that she had any special reason to expect trouble, but it was always possible. She was visiting the parents of a boy already on her books, and she had some bad news to deliver.

She passed another couple of doors before reaching the correct flat, then rang the bell. Hearing sounds of movement from inside, she waited a minute or so, but no one appeared. She tried again, ringing longer, and this time she heard a shouted curse followed by heavy footsteps approaching the door.

'Yes?' An angry face confronted her. It belonged to the father of the house, and, from his bleary eyes and uncombed hair, he'd just been woken up from an afternoon nap.

'Mr Dickinson?' she enquired politely.

'Who wants to know?' was growled back at her.

'Mrs Peters, Social Services,' she informed him, at the same time holding up her identity card. 'I telephoned your wife earlier.'

'Well, the cow's not home,' he announced, and would have slammed the door if Sara hadn't inserted an experienced foot.

'Mr Dickinson, I've come to talk about Wayne,' she went on determinedly, and at his blank, boozy stare felt the need to say, 'Your son Wayne, Mr Dickinson.'

'I know who the little sod is,' he muttered, his voice definitely drink-slurred. 'He's not here, either.'

'I realise that, Mr Dickinson,' Sara replied patiently. 'That's why I've come. I have some rather distressing news.'

This, at last, got his attention, as he demanded, 'Not dead, is he?'

'Oh, no!' Sara hastened to inform him. 'He's all right, physically. However, I'm afraid he was caught breaking and entering last night.'

This news neither surprised nor particularly disturbed his father. 'Well, what do you want me to do about it?' he asked truculently.

'I thought you'd want to know, so you can go and visit him. He's presently at the Youth Centre in——' Sara wasn't allowed to finish.

'Visit him? Why the hell should I? He never visits me when I'm in the nick,' his father complained.

Sara wondered if he could possibly be serious. His sullen look suggested he was. Still, she had to pursue it.

'Mr Dickinson, Wayne needs all the support he can get. I know this is his second offence——'

'Third,' he corrected, 'and I never got nothing from them, neither. Cigarette warehouse was the last one, and did he give me one bloody packet? Not one! He's a wrong 'un, all right,' his father denounced in an almost pious tone.

Sara decided that, unbelievable as it seemed, he *was* quite serious. Apparently his son's meanness counted as a bigger crime than his dishonesty. She knew from that point on it was a matter of going through the motions.

'Mr Dickinson, I hope you'll reconsider. He's now too old to be treated as a juvenile, but we could possibly get him out on bail. Then we could try for community work rather than a custodial sentence, but a judge will expect home support,' she explained, already knowing from his glassy look that he'd lost interest. 'If you effectively disown him——'

'That's it. That's what I'll do,' Dickinson cut in, relishing the phrase she'd unintentionally supplied. 'I'm disowning him. Should have done it years ago.'

Sighing inwardly, Sara decided it was time for retreat. 'All right, Mr Dickinson, but is there any message you wish me to pass on to Wayne?'

'Yes, you tell him not to come back here when he gets out—the sod. Do you understand?'

'Perfectly,' Sara answered, disgust rather than fear uppermost. 'However, if you change your mind——'

'I won't, so you can just clear off, too!' he shouted at her through beer fumes.

'Very well, Mr Dickinson.' Sara deliberately ignored the abuse. 'Let me say your candour has been most refreshing, and I must agree it would not be in Wayne's interest to return to such an environment. I can only pray I won't have to inconvenience you again.'

'Wot?' This time Dickinson's jaw dropped open in a vacuous expression.

Sara was already walking off, along the balcony, before he realised there had been sarcasm behind her speech. Then he shouted after her, 'Go to hell, you hear me? Nosy bitch! Someone should give you one. That'll show you.'

Sara didn't bother looking back. She'd heard it all before.

But she'd forgotten Neville waiting patiently along the balcony. He'd heard the shouting and had begun to walk rapidly towards her.

'What's going on?' he asked, his eyes ranging past her to take in the character in the doorway.

'I'd give you one myself...' Dickinson was just adding, when he noticed she was no longer alone.

Wisely he tailed off, but it was already too late. Neville had brushed off Sara's hand and was striding along the balcony. He was so quick, Dickinson was still considering his next move when he was seized by the collar and slammed against the door.

'Hey, mister——' he protested on a frightened note.

'You'd do what?' Neville demanded, livid with anger.

'I...n-nothing, m-mister,' a helpless Dickinson stammered. 'I didn't mean nothing.'

'Neville!' Sara cried out, trying in vain to drag him away. 'Leave it, please.'

Neville didn't seem to hear, as he shifted his grip to the man's neck, growling, 'Apologise, you fat pig!'

'I——' Dickinson could hardly find breath to apologise.

But Neville didn't let up, squeezing harder as he repeated, *'Apologise!'*

'OK! OK! I apologise,' the other man gasped out, then blubbered, 'Please, mister, let me go. You're choking me.'

This wasn't far from the truth, his face having turned a bright shade of red. Neville, however, seemed oblivious as once more Sara tried to pull him off.

'Please, stop it,' she begged him, her own face white at the violence. 'Please, Neville—for me.'

Her distress finally got through to him, as, slowly, he released his hold. Perhaps he saw Dickinson as the pathetic character he really was. At any rate, he gave him a last look of contempt, and made to walk away with Sara.

It was she who noticed Dickinson's arm rising as Neville turned his back, and she who shouted a warning. The other man still managed to strike a glancing blow while Neville wheeled round. It didn't seem to have much effect, however, as Neville responded with a punch on the jaw that dropped the flabby, half-drunk Dickinson to the ground. He didn't follow up on it, but instead hurried Sara away from the scene.

He held on to her as they descended in the lift, and a badly shaken Sara took deep, calming breaths.

'I'm OK,' she said, when she'd half recovered her nerve. 'I just hate that sort of thing.'

'I'm not much of a fighter, either.' He pulled a face that suggested he felt no pride in beating the other man. 'It was just the way he talked to you.'

'Par for the course.' Sara shrugged off what was quite normal abuse, but she felt no anger towards Neville. If anyone was to blame, it was she for taking him there.

He frowned. 'You're *serious*? People usually speak to you like that?'

Sara nodded, and couldn't resist saying, 'You weren't so polite yourself, if you remember.'

'No, I suppose I wasn't,' he admitted, and actually looked guilty for once.

'How's your head?' Sara asked, changing the subject. 'Where he hit you, I mean.'

'I'll survive,' he replied, as the lift hit bottom and he helped her out. 'It's you I'm worried about.'

'Well, don't be,' she dismissed. 'I can cope. Sticks and stones may break my bones, et cetera. If I were you, I'd concentrate on worrying about your car.'

This, she added, as they emerged from the flats to find the car still there but the youths disappeared. There was no evident damage until they were alongside it. Then they couldn't miss the gaping hole in the facia where the stereo had been, and the open glove compartment. The final insult was a note glued with chewing-gum to the dashboard. It read, 'Thanks for the watch—reel clasy.'

Wordlessly, Neville detached the note and screwed it into a ball, before unlocking the car and climbing in. Sara was left to follow suit.

After a moment or two, she dared to ask, 'There was a watch in the glove compartment?'

He nodded. 'A Rolex—"reel clasy", to quote our illiterate note-writer.'

'Oh.' Sara had a general idea of the price range and lapsed into a respectful silence.

'Aren't you going to say "I told you so"?' Neville muttered, as he set the car in motion.

'Would you like me to?'

'Not particularly.'

Sara took the hint and asked instead, 'Will your insurance cover it?'

'It should.' He nodded. 'At any rate, I'll have to buy a replacement. It was for Scott's birthday.'

'Oh, when is it?' Sara smiled at this mention of the boy.

'Tomorrow. I thought you might like to come to the school with me, and take him out for lunch,' he suggested casually.

It was his very casualness that took Sara's breath away. He dropped out of her life, then dropped in again, just when it suited him.

'Is that silence favourable or unfavourable?' he said after a moment.

'Unfavourable,' Sara replied shortly. 'So you can let me out here. I'll get a bus from this stop,' she added, hoping to avoid another argument. From memory, she always ended up losing them.

Neville, however, chose to ignore the request, saying, 'I suppose you've wondered where I've been for the last month.'

'No... Should I have?' she retorted.

'Well, that's me put in my place.' He sounded more amused than angry. 'Nevertheless, for the record, I had to go to the States to promote a film.'

'Really?' an indifferent Sara muttered.

'Yes, *really*,' he echoed, 'and the whole thing was exceedingly boring.'

'All work and no play, you mean?' She gave him a sceptical look, imagining he hadn't been short of female company.

It was a mistake as he rounded with, 'Not jealous, are we?'

'No, we are not!' she almost shouted back.

His smile didn't falter. 'Good, because you have no reason to be,' he assured. 'You see, Mrs Peters, believe it or not, I found myself spending an alarming amount of time thinking about you.'

Sara didn't believe it. 'That's why you telephoned so often, I suppose,' she said in a sarcastic vein.

'Yes, well...' he hesitated, as if searching for an excuse, and came up with '... I assumed you'd probably put the phone down on me. Wouldn't you?'

He was quite possibly right but Sara still said, 'That's hardly the point.'

'I only get credit if I did phone, is that it?' he challenged.

'Yes...no...this is silly.' Sara wondered why she was letting herself be drawn into this. 'Seriously, I have some shopping to do, if I want to eat tonight. So could you please drop me off?'

'I'll come with you—carry your parcels as an act of contrition,' he suggested, throwing her his most charming smile.

'I'm just buying groceries,' she stated, 'and I have no desire to be mobbed by your adoring public while I do so.'

'In that case,' he countered, 'we'd better eat out. Where do you fancy?'

'I don't,' she said flatly. 'Apart from the fact I'm not dressed for dining out, I'd prefer a quiet night in.'

'All right,' he agreed.

It seemed too easy to Sara, this sudden capitulation. She expected some devious move, and was not disappointed as he began heading towards the river.

'We're going in the wrong direction,' she pointed out, quite unnecessarily she was sure.

'You said you wanted a quiet evening in, you don't want my so-called adoring public mobbing us, and you look too tired to cook, anyway. So I've decided that dinner at my place is the ideal solution,' he said as if it were all perfectly reasonable.

'I don't suppose it's occurred to you to consult me,' she objected.

'As a matter of fact, it did,' he claimed, 'but as you'd probably have said "no", I decided not to risk it. Was I correct?'

'Absolutely,' Sara confirmed shortly, but didn't bother pursuing the argument. For he was right on another point. She was tired—too tired to argue irrelevancies.

And that was what she would have been doing, when she already knew he was going to get his own way. He always did.

Always. That evening, when somehow he made her relax and enjoy dinner at his place. And later, as he drove her home, he managed to talk her into travelling down to Kent to take Scott out to celebrate his birthday.

Then, in the weeks that followed, there were the dinner dates and the party invitations he bullied and cajoled her into accepting. Three times a week she saw him. Sometimes she had prior warning, via the telephone. Others, he would simply arrive on her doorstep, turn a deaf ear to her protests and whisk her away somewhere.

Arguably, she didn't have to go. She could have refused, and kept on refusing, no matter how much he wore her down. But how much easier it was just to go along. Let him take her out, and amuse her with that clever sense of humour, and make her forget the cares of the world for a while, so that she found she tackled her work with renewed optimism.

He asked nothing in return. Once in a while, he'd take her hand or put a casual arm round her shoulder. And at times he'd look at her as if he wanted to do more. But he never did. When they danced now, it was with a respectable gap between them. When they said good-night, it was with a chaste peck on the cheek. So why should she object?

If she was the one wanting more, she never admitted it. Instead she told lies to Bob and Kathy, and to her friends at work, and most of all to herself. She pretended that it was a simple friendship, no more. Any other feelings she ignored—like the rush of pleasure each time she saw him again, the longing she suffered each time he left, without touching or holding or kissing her. She barely noticed that Nick was receding in the past.

And, through it all, she still believed she was in control of her life. Fool that she was!

CHAPTER TEN

IT WAS Easter when things finally caught up with Sara. She'd booked a few days' holiday, and planned to spend it with her parents. She hadn't visited them since Christmas and they'd begun to ask gently curious questions about why she was so often out when they phoned at night. She hadn't mentioned Neville. She was fairly sure they wouldn't approve and she thought it easier to just keep the two parts of her life separate.

Unfortunately, Neville did not share her view. When he discovered she was going down to Kent the day before he collected Scott for the holidays, he decided to drive her down and stay in a hotel overnight. That way, she'd be saved a train journey and he'd get to meet her parents.

With visions of Neville at his most extreme and her father at his most conservative, the idea horrified her. But, short of telling the truth—that her parents would have an apoplexy if she brought *him* home—she couldn't find any excuse that didn't sound lame. Even if she'd come up with a good one, it was debatable whether he would have listened. *He* had decided—for his own reasons—that he was going to drive her home, and drive her home he would!

Why she put up with his high-handedness Sara didn't know, but, as they drew up outside the gates of her parents' house, she wished that, for once, she'd stood her ground.

'Here?' Neville repeated, as he stared at the high gates that hinted at the sizeable property behind. Whatever he had expected from her home, it wasn't this.

160

'I'll go,' she said, slipping out to open the gates and waiting till he'd driven through to shut them.

She climbed into the car again, and watched his eyes widen further as they approached the Tudor elegance of her family home.

'It's called Orchards,' she said, a note of pride in her voice.

'It's beautiful,' he said with genuine admiration. 'I thought you said your father worked in an office.'

'He does,' she insisted.

'What kind of office? The Home Office? The Foreign Office?'

'No, he works in a stockbroker's office,' she said, still not fully confessing the truth.

But Neville guessed, 'I imagine from this place he *is* the office.'

'Well, yes,' she conceded, 'the firm is called Summerfield, Summerfield and Carter.'

'Who's the second Summerfield—your chess-playing brother?' he asked, surprising Sara with his good memory.

'No, it was my father originally, the first Summerfield being my grandpa. My brother's a doctor,' she added without thinking.

'Like your husband.' Neville's lips thinned slightly.

'Yes, they were interns at the same hospital,' she explained briefly, then ran on, 'Look, you don't have to come in. I won't consider it rude if you just cut and run.'

'No, but *I* will,' he said, already climbing out of the car.

She followed him, just as her mother appeared in the doorway.

Her heart sank as she waited for her mother's reaction. She still hadn't told her parents about Neville—she'd hoped for a last-minute reprieve.

The first thing that struck her was her mother's *lack* of reaction. In the three years she'd been a widow, Sara had never brought anybody home. Yet her mother showed no surprise at her arriving with a male stranger in tow. Instead she came up to greet her with a kiss on the cheek, then turned to await an introduction.

Sara performed it quickly, making an indistinct mutter of Neville's surname and simply calling him an acquaintance.

Her mother extended a polite hand and a pleasant smile, and Sara thought she'd got away with it.

Her mother said, 'Nice to meet you, Mr Dryden.'

And he corrected, 'Neville, please.'

'All right, *Neville*,' her mother agreed with a smile, before going on, 'I've been looking forward to meeting you. You will stay for afternoon tea, I hope?'

'Love to.' Neville smiled back, and took Sara's arm as they all walked inside.

Sara said nothing; she was too confused. How could her mother *look forward* to meeting somebody she hadn't known existed?

Things were much the same when they entered the morning-room to find her father reading the paper. He stood up and greeted them both, showing only slightly more surprise than his wife.

It was then that Sara realised her parents had, at the very least, known she was seeing someone. It took her a little longer to realise they also knew exactly who Neville was. This she gathered when her father *didn't* ask him what he did for a living—usually his first question of a stranger—and behaved in an unusually re-strained manner towards his guest.

This didn't seem to bother Neville. He, in turn, be-haved in a respectful manner towards the older man, and made no attempts to charm or impress him. Afternoon tea was an almost formal affair; if hardly a success, at least not the disaster Sara had predicted, and she was happy to leave things that way.

In fact, conversation had pretty much dried up when Neville, looking for a safe topic, alighted on the one thing guaranteed to warm up her father—antiques.

'I see you're a collector,' he said, nodding towards a set of snuff boxes arranged on the mantelpiece—and that was enough.

Soon they were engaged in a discussion of the merits of the various pieces, as her father handed each to Neville, who examined them with suitable care and reverence, and asked all the right-sounding questions about date and origin. After that, Sara and her mother might as well have not been there.

From snuff boxes, they progressed to chess sets and, before Sara knew it, her father had whipped Neville off to the inner sanctum of his study.

'Thank God for that,' Elaine Summerfield said when the two men had gone.

'For what?' Sara frowned.

'They like each other, I think,' her mother announced with evident relief.

It certainly seemed that way, and Sara supposed she should have been relieved, too, but a little bit of her resented the ease with which her father had been won over.

'I wasn't sure they would,' her mother continued. 'I mean, when Simon told us you were seeing him, dear——'

'Simon told you?' Sara repeated sharply.

Her mother looked a little apologetic, before explaining, 'Apparently he called at the house a couple of weeks ago, and Kathy told him you were out with Neville.'

'And he passed the news on,' Sara concluded.

Nodding, her mother said gently, 'I hope you don't mind, dear. I know you value your privacy, but Simon felt we'd be interested.'

Sara shrugged. It was too late now to mind. She just wondered what brother Simon thought of it all.

As things transpired, she didn't have to wait long to find out. After showing Neville every antique in the house, her father insisted on his staying to dinner, and before Sara could call a halt her mother was making a family occasion of it by inviting Simon and his wife. With an au pair to baby-sit the children, they accepted the invitation quite readily.

By this time, Sara felt matters were totally beyond her control. Her earlier concern over her parents' disapproval had turned into annoyance at the effortless way Neville had ingratiated himself. She might have known that, being a woman, her mother might be susceptible to the Dryden charm, but she had expected more of her father. Instead he, too, seemed taken in, as the two shared an aperitif and chatted with the ease of long acquaintance.

It was only later, when her brother and his wife arrived, that things didn't quite go Neville's way. Marge he succeeded in charming almost immediately, but Simon definitely didn't share her enthusiasm.

Not that he was blatant about it. He talked in a fairly civil manner, and a stranger certainly wouldn't have noticed anything amiss. But Sara did. She knew Simon too well to be deceived by his neutral tones. Each time she caught his eye over the dinner table, there was a question in it—a question she wasn't going to be allowed to avoid.

While her father invited Neville to sample his best brandy, Simon almost dragged her away for a walk in the garden.

They'd barely stepped out of the french doors when he pounced on her. 'Well?'

Sara feigned ignorance. 'Well, what?'

'Come on, Sis. You stay away for months, are rarely in when I call, and then you turn up, out of the blue, with this chap in tow.' Her brother made no attempt to hide his disapproval.

'I haven't been staying away,' she protested. 'I've been busy, that's all.'

'So I gathered,' Simon countered, a reference to Neville's clear indications over dinner of how often they saw each other. 'You could have told us about him, couldn't you? All right, I know you're a grown-up, independent woman, and you're not answerable to your family any more. But dammit, Sis, we do care about you... And, whether you want to face it or not, that chap's completely out of your league!'

It was nothing Sara hadn't told herself a dozen times, but that didn't mean she wanted to hear it from anyone else, including her brother.

'What do you know about it?' She rounded on him. 'Honestly, Simon, you have a nerve. If I want to go out with Neville, it's my business. No one else's.'

'I appreciate that, but——'

'No buts, Simon. I don't need your permission to see anyone.'

'I realise that.' Her brother held his hands up in truce. 'I just don't want to see you hurt.'

'Well, thanks for the concern,' Sara responded, scarcely pacified, 'but I'm perfectly capable of handling the situation.'

'Are you, Sis?' Simon gave her a worried look. 'Have you any idea of what kind of man he is? How many women there have been in his life?'

'No, but then I don't waste my time scouring gossip columns—and I'm rather surprised you do,' she said with some disdain.

'I don't normally,' Simon denied. 'I made it my business to find out about him, that's all. And there's no way he's right for you, Sara.'

'Oh, really?' she said in sarcastic tones.

'Yes, really,' he continued, regardless. 'Look, I can understand your being attracted to him, on a physical level, and if you're simply sleeping with him——'

'You'll give me your blessing?' she cut in again, her anger growing. 'Well, I'll remember that, brother dear, *if* and *when* he asks me.'

'You mean——?' Her brother stopped in his tracks, as he realised he'd jumped the gun.

'Yes,' she said flatly. 'Though it still isn't any of your business.'

'OK, perhaps not,' he finally conceded, although he couldn't resist adding, 'He's just not the sort of man I'd have picked for you.'

'No, he's not,' Sara agreed meaningfully.

But Simon was oblivious, as he went on, 'And you have to admit he's very different from Nick.'

Sara frowned at the mention of her husband. Lately she hadn't thought too much of Nick, and she had no wish to go into comparisons now. It was unfair of her brother to try and use him like this.

'So?' She shrugged back. 'I'm not looking for a replacement for Nick, you know.'

'Just as well,' Simon muttered in response.

Sara could have left it, but irritation made her challenge, 'What's that supposed to mean?'

'Come on, Sis——' Simon raised an exasperated eyebrow '—he might be charming enough, your actor friend, and he might have won Dad round, but you know perfectly well he's not half the man Nick——'

'*Simon!*' she broke in, anger rising.

'What?'

'I suggest you shut up now.'

'But——' About to go on, her brother finally realised he'd overstepped the mark.

Sara felt a rare hostility towards him. She turned to re-enter the house, then noticed Neville standing at the french windows. Her heart sank as she wondered how much he'd heard.

All of it, it seemed, as he said, 'Why tell him to shut up, Sara? It's what you think, too, isn't it? That I'm not half the man your husband was.'

'Neville, I . . .' She trailed off, too embarrassed to say more in front of her brother.

It was Simon who explained, quite unnecessarily, 'Look, Dryden, you weren't meant to overhear——'

'Obviously,' Neville inserted coldly.

'Then don't take it out on Sara,' her brother continued. 'I was the one expressing doubts about her relationship with you. She hasn't said a word.'

'She doesn't have to,' Neville responded, his eyes still fixed on Sara. 'Her silence speaks volumes,' he added.

'Neville, please——' She laid an appealing hand on his arm.

It was shrugged off. 'Don't bother. I can see myself out. You may thank your parents for their hospitality.'

For an instant Sara was taken by surprise as he turned on his heel, but when she understood he was walking out she moved quickly enough.

'Neville——' She caught up with him in the hall, and stood in front of the door to block his exit. 'Please, listen——'

'Why?' he demanded with the same coldness. 'I think your brother said it all, don't you?'

'I know how it must have sounded.' She made an apologetic face. 'It's just that Simon thinks you might hurt me.'

'What?' His tone changed to one of incredulity. 'Hurt you? Hell, most of the time I can't get close enough to touch, far less hurt.'

'I meant emotionally,' she stated.

'So did I,' he countered, and his eyes revealed a bitterness long suppressed. 'I don't know why I ever bothered. I knew from the start I was never going to match up to the dear departed,' he said almost brutally.

'Don't!' Sara protested, but to no avail.

'After all, how could I?' he ran on. 'Competing against a normal man would have been bad enough, but a saint——'

'That's not fair!' she retorted. 'I've never spoken about Nick.'

He gave an unpleasant laugh. 'You didn't need to *talk* about him, *darling*. Not when his bloody picture's all over your flat!'

'That's rubbish!' Sara snapped, any idea of apologising rapidly fading.

'Oh, is it?' he grated back. 'What about the wedding photograph on the mantelpiece? Or the graduation one on the sideboard? Not to mention, of course, the silver-framed effort by the bedside.'

'How do you...?' Sara was puzzled how he knew of the last.

'One time I was allowed in for coffee, I had a look,' he said without apology. 'It was hardly a surprise, though. In fact, I'm willing to bet the locket you always wear also holds a likeness of the good doctor.'

Sara blushed at the truth of this. Until now, she hadn't even considered that these photographs might bother him.

On the defensive, she retorted, 'What if it does? It has nothing to do with you.'

'No, it doesn't, does it? How stupid of me to think it might have,' Neville muttered angrily, and, before she could stop him, reached to open the door.

Sara found herself running after him again, this time catching him at the car. It was still parked in the fore-court, now lit by overhead lights.

'You don't understand,' she claimed in an almost whining tone.

'No,' he conceded bitterly, 'but then I couldn't be expected to. After all, what do I know about love—at least, the pure variety you and Saint Nick practised?' he added on a note of cruel mockery.

Too much for Sara, she raised a hand and struck him across the face. A resounding slap, it took him by surprise and jerked his head backwards.

For a moment they stood in silence, rocked by the violence of her action. Then Neville grabbed her, dragging her into his arms and ignoring her cry of fright as he kissed her with the same angry passion that had motivated her slap.

That was the way it began—her struggling, him hurting—an explosion of frustration and anger. She lashed out with her hands, and they were forced behind her back. She tried to kick and he pushed her hard against the car. She twisted her head to the side but he lifted his other hand to grab a handful of hair and make her accept the kiss.

So when did it change? When she became tired of struggling, and resistance drained away? Or when his desire to hurt became a different kind of desire, and the hands that trapped her gradually lost their roughness, and began to hold her, caress her, until her body, too, began to betray her, as all the emotion, suppressed till now, came in a rush. Instead of struggling, she turned in his arms to press closer and closer, while her lips lifted to his, opening, responding, promising everything.

It was Neville who finally drew back, and, although his breathing was as uneven as her own, he looked at her with such coldness.

Sara knew she had to make the first overture. Finding no words, she reached to touch the cheek she'd slapped.

The gesture was not understood, as he lifted a hand to grasp hers and push it away.

'No more games, Sara,' he muttered harshly, and, with a last bitter stare, turned to climb into his car.

Sara stood watching him, feeling helpless. It wasn't until he started the engine that she cried, 'Neville, please wait!'

The appeal seemed to go unheard. He reversed the Daimler, throwing up gravel as he accelerated down the driveway. Sara was left staring after him, praying he would change his mind and return.

Of course he didn't. He didn't even look back.

Sara continued to stand there, not noticing the light rain that had begun to fall. She did not cry. She was beyond tears. The game was over and she'd lost.

So why had she ever played it? What arrogance had made her imagine she'd be able to walk away and not look back? That was his role; he'd been playing it all his life. While she, she'd always been cast to have the broken heart. Such an over-used phrase—a broken heart—but that was how it felt, this ache inside.

Only now, as she watched his tail-lights disappear, did Sara realise how foolish she'd been. She'd thought she could control both him and her feelings. She'd thought she could stop herself caring, simply by knowing it was unwise. And, along the way, all the signs she'd ignored, all the lies she'd told herself, in a refusal to face the truth...

God help her, but she loved him.

CHAPTER ELEVEN

EVENTUALLY Sara's mother came out to drape a coat over her shoulders, saying gently, 'Simon's told me what happened. Did you sort things out with Neville?'

Sara shook her head and answered simply, 'No, Mother, it's all over.'

She revealed little of the hurt she felt, but Elaine Summerfield had seen that remote look in her eyes before. The last time she'd let herself be excluded from her daughter's grief. This time she wasn't going to just stand by.

'Here!' She produced a set of car keys from her own coat. 'Go after him.'

Sara stared at her mother in puzzlement. Hadn't she heard? It was over.

'Do you love him?' her mother asked bluntly.

And Sara found herself answering in the same vein, 'Yes—yes, I do.'

Her mother said no more. Sara understood. It was up to her. If she loved him, she'd go after him.

Sara thought no further as she took the keys and pressed her mother's hand, before hurrying round the house to the converted stables where her mother's car was garaged.

It was an act of faith, driving to Neville's hotel, without any idea of what she was going to do or say. Quite calmly she waited at the reception, while a desk clerk rang his room and discovered that Mr Dryden was available. She had no doubts until a porter escorted her to the room on the second floor, then discreetly withdrew.

171

She knocked softly on the door. There was no response. She knocked a little harder.

'It's open,' an impatient voice called from the other side. It was hardly encouraging.

She took a deep breath, and, pushing open the door, walked inside.

At first the room seemed empty. It was lit only by a bedside lamp and she could barely see him, sitting in shadow, in an armchair by the far corner. She gave a little start when he spoke.

'I suppose you've come for your bag,' he muttered at her.

For a moment Sara was at a loss. She'd forgotten the weekend case he'd brought down for her. 'My bag, yes,' she echoed, grateful for the excuse.

'A porter carried it up with mine.' He nodded towards the two cases stacked on a rack by the window.

Sara came a little further into the room, then hesitated. Her bag was on the far side of the bed and she would have to step over Neville's outstretched legs to get there. She waited instead for him to make some move.

He took his time, draining the drink he'd been nursing before he got to his feet to pick up her bag and walk round to her side of the bed.

'I may as well carry it downstairs for you,' he said less than graciously.

Sara shook her head. 'Don't bother. I'll manage.'

'Suit yourself.' He shrugged as if it didn't matter to him either way.

But, when Sara stretched out a hand to take the case, he kept hold of it, and fixed chilling blue eyes on her. It was then she realised that, beneath his pretence of indifference, he was still angry, very angry indeed. Possibly it was just his pride that was hurt, but she didn't want things to end on this bitter note.

'Look, Neville,' she began softly, 'I am sorry about tonight. My brother shouldn't have said what he did, but you must understand it wasn't personal to you.'

'Wasn't it?' He looked sceptical.

'No, honestly,' she insisted. 'He was just being protective.'

'Really?' he responded, this time with a decidedly bored air, and Sara gave up.

She took a last look at his arrogant yet beautiful face, snatched the case from his hand, and walked away. Her hand was on the doorknob when his voice called her back.

'Then he was the same with your husband?' he demanded in harsher tones that cut through the pretence of indifference.

Sara turned slowly and let her case drop to the floor, as she searched for the right answer. Only there wasn't one—unless she was prepared to lie.

She didn't have to. He concluded for himself, 'No, of course not. Your brother thought the good doctor was a saint too, did he?'

Sara flinched at the contempt in his voice. 'Don't start that again, Neville,' she said almost wearily.

'Why? A sacrilege, is it?' He made a scornful sound.

'Neville, please . . .' Sara didn't want to fight.

'Please, what?' He raised a sarcastic brow. 'Surely I can talk *about* the man, even if I'm not fit to fill his shoes—or his bed.'

The last Sara couldn't ignore. If he'd been trying to goad her, he'd succeeded.

'All right, Neville, what do you want?' She took an angry step towards him. 'Do you want to know what my husband was really like? Is that it?'

Although she'd asked the question, it surprised Sara when he answered, 'Yes. Yes, I do. I'm sick of dancing round the subject, sick of going on dates and having him look over my shoulder all the time.'

'Oh, that's absurd!' Sara snapped in return. 'Perhaps I am sensitive, but it's taken me a while to get over his death. And I'm not going to lie to please you, either. Yes, I admired my husband—I admired him very much. But he was no saint.

'He could be incredibly bloody-minded when he chose, he'd little time for people he believed stupid, and he was so proud of being working class, he felt it gave him automatic rights to be rude to anyone who wasn't,' Sara said, with absolute frankness, then, seeing Neville was still listening, she ran on, 'As for being a *good doctor*, he *was* considered an excellent diagnostician, but he had a most appalling bedside manner. If he'd lived, he'd most probably have gone in for research... And that's about it,' she finished abruptly.

She felt she'd said enough. In trying to be honest, she hadn't been quite fair to Nick, but it was hard to explain the sometimes difficult, sometimes wonderful man her husband had been.

Neville still wasn't satisfied, and asked the one thing that she'd missed out. 'Did you love him?'

Sara did not hesitate. 'Yes, I loved him,' she answered simply.

'And now?' he pursued.

Sara didn't know what to say. Till recently, she hadn't accepted Nick's death. A part of her had been waiting for some dreadful mistake to be corrected and for him to return. Her life certainly hadn't moved forward. But now?

Nick Peters had dominated the beginning of her adult life and all her memories weren't going to suddenly disappear. But they hadn't stopped her loving Neville. She looked at him now and felt an almost frightening love for him.

'What do you want from me, Neville?' she finally said.

'You know,' he responded.

He was right, of course. She knew. She'd known for a long time. He wanted her. Not forever. Maybe not for more than one night. He wanted her and he'd never pretended otherwise.

It was she who had pretended, she who had imagined they could be just friends, ignoring the powerful attraction that lay between them. Only now was the time of reckoning.

Now, as their eyes caught and held and he looked at her with such desire she felt it like a caress. Now, as he walked slowly towards her and made her heart beat so hard it hurt. Yet she didn't try to run away, but waited for him, trembling a little as he reached out to cup her cheek.

'And you want me. You know that, too,' he claimed, his eyes still holding hers.

Sara tried to deny it, but she couldn't. Her breath caught as his hand trailed downwards to the base of her throat and slowly pushed open the shirt-dress below her coat. Her lips moved soundlessly as his fingers spread against the first swell of her breast, barely covered by the camisole she wore beneath. She tried to step back then, but his other arm went round her waist to draw her to him, and, before she could protest, his mouth covered hers.

He kissed her gently at first, his lips barely brushing hers, and all thought of resistance just faded away. The hand she lifted to push at him curled round his neck instead, and, feeling her responsiveness, he gradually deepened the kiss until she opened her lips to his, allowing him to taste the sweet intimacy of her mouth. They had kissed before, but never like this, with no attempt to hide feelings, no wish to keep control, and desire flowed between them like a river in flood.

Sara made no protest as his hand pushed further into her dress, forcing open the buttons, sliding over silk to cup the fullness of a breast, which was already straining for his hold. Then, growing impatient, he pulled apart the front lacing of her camisole so he could touch her bare flesh, and she whimpered with shock and pleasure as his fingers closed over the peak of her breast. She felt herself slipping, falling into some dark place beyond reason, and the fear returned, making her twist away from him.

Breathing hard, they stared at each other, frustration in Neville's eyes, panic in hers. She took another step back and he caught her arm.

'It's all right,' he said, misreading her actions. 'Don't be scared. I'd never force you.'

Sara shook her head, trying to tell him he hadn't understood. She wasn't afraid of his lovemaking, but of laying herself open to the hurt that would follow. The inevitable hurt when one day—tomorrow, or next week, or next month—he tired of her.

With no idea of her thoughts, Neville saw only the anguish he'd caused.

In a gesture more loving than sexual, he touched the back of his hand to her cheek, saying, 'You'd better go.'

'Yes,' Sara agreed softly. She had to go, before love overcame fear, and tied her to him with a bond she'd never break.

'Now, Sara!' he added, his voice harshening, barely in control.

But it was already too late, Sara realised. She stood before him, unable to go, already tied. 'I can't,' she said in an almost soundless whisper, while her eyes betrayed the love that held her there.

He didn't seem to notice, as he rasped, 'Don't play games with me, Sara Peters. Not unless you know the rules.'

'I do.' Sara knew them well enough—no promises, no commitments—but such were her feelings for him, she was willing to accept so little.

She looked at him steadily, and eventually he reached for her again. He held her at arm's length as if he expected her to take flight. When she didn't, he drew her closer until their bodies touched and she felt the beat of his heart matching the beat of her own. If he didn't love her, he wanted her, and that was as much as she would get. It had to be enough.

He held her to him for a moment, his lips pressed to her brow, and when he felt her tremble again, he urged, 'Trust me. I'll make it right for you...so right.'

The intensity in his voice unnerved her more, but she willed herself to stop trembling, as he slipped off her raincoat, and, draping it over her case, took her hand. He led her away from the door, towards the bed.

He did not talk again, as he started to undress her. He did it without fuss, gathering her dark copper hair so that it fell down her back, before unbuttoning the front of her shirt-dress. Then, eyes fixed on her, he backed away and waited.

Sara realised what he was waiting for. He did not want a passive partner. She wasn't going to be allowed to lie to herself, and pretend he'd seduced her. She had to come to him willingly.

It was Sara's choice and the woman in her overcame the girl, as she slipped off the dress and let it fall to the floor.

A satisfied sound escaped Neville's lips, before the sight of her completely took his breath away. His eyes went to the soft swell of her breasts, barely encased in a white silk camisole, then they moved down, over the lace-edged briefs covering her hips, to her long, shapely legs.

When his eyes eventually switched back to her face, it was to see a certain shyness there. He knew, without being told, that he would be the only one, apart from her husband. Yet he still minded. He could have accepted other affairs; he'd had enough himself. It was the

love he minded, the love she'd given the younger man—
so much love, it had long outlasted his death. And,
though she was here now, Neville felt he was no more
than a substitute. It was a bitter thing to face, a thing
pride would once have made him reject.

But he had no pride any more. Not when it came to
this girl. And, if she never loved him, he knew he could
make her his in other ways.

Unable to read his thoughts, Sara saw only calcu-
lation in his dark blue eyes. It made her shiver, but she
stood her ground as he unbuttoned his shirt to reveal a
muscular chest covered in dark hair. He threw the shirt
on the bed, before closing the gap between them, and,
holding her gaze, lifted a hand to unlace the front of
her camisole. He did it without touching her, the ties
already loose enough to come away easily. When it
parted, his eyes switched from her face to her full breasts,
spilling out from the silk. And it was his eyes that ca-
ressed her, as he drew the garment from her shoulders
and let it drop to the floor.

Then he reached for her, his hands smoothing over
her naked back while his head bent to kiss the soft skin
at her throat, and Sara gave a low moan of pleasure at
the gentle bite of his lips, the rough caress of his hands.

Desire grew from longing to pain, and she twisted in
his arms, drawing a groan from Neville as he felt her
warm breasts swelling against his chest. He raised his
head and, hungrily covering her mouth, lifted her body
to his.

Beyond thought or fear, Sara's senses reeled at the
touch of him, and the smell of him, and his sheer, overpowering maleness. She clung to him as he turned her
in his arms. She went with him as he pressed her down
on the bed.

Then his lips left hers and trailed in a slow path downwards, lingering at the pulse at the base of her throat,
before moving on, tasting the light sweat on her skin,

touching the swell of her breast, moving on, until they finally found what they sought. And Sara cried aloud as he reached the peak and took the nipple in his mouth, slowly circling it with his tongue, gently sucking, then bringing it to full life as he began to pull hungrily at her flesh.

She arched to him in sweet agony, then lifted his head away, only to offer her other breast, aching for his touch.

He took it willingly, pleasuring both of them with the bite and play of his mouth—until he needed more. Raising his head from her breast, he pressed her back on the bed and slid a hand over her stomach to the silk of her briefs. He felt her tense, but it did not stop him. Gently pushing them away, he smoothed his hands over her legs and drew down her stockings, to leave her quite naked.

That done, he rose from the bed and stood before her, uttering a ragged, 'Don't!' when she made to cover herself, compelling her to let him look, to tell her with his eyes how beautiful he found her, hair falling across her breasts, lips moist and parted, waiting for him. Then he covered her himself, before he began to remove his own clothing.

Sara watched him with wide, glazed eyes and felt a renewed sense of panic. But it stilled the moment he lay down beside her and kissed her softly on the mouth, before drawing his hand over her body again. He cupped her breast, and gently traced the nipple, then slipped downwards, spreading his palm against the flat of her stomach, rousing in her a sweet ache that wanted him to touch the dark, intimate place he sought. Needed him to, as she let him part her thighs and gave a startled sob at the first sensual stroke of his fingers.

He pleasured her until she arched her body to his. Then, knowing she was ready for him and feeling his own control slipping, he lifted himself above her. He watched her eyes widen as he poised to possess her, then thrust himself into her, claiming her as his, claiming it for all time.

Sara felt the same way, as love and desire fused together into one. When he began moving inside her, she reached for him, lifting her body to his, gasping at the pleasure it gave.

And each time he took her, Neville felt stronger, more powerful, driven by the sweetness of her response. He knew then he'd never really made love before. Not like this, not with every part of him alive and wanting her. Wanting her even as she cried out to him, and he held her, and spilled his seed into her, calling her name.

Even as they lay together afterwards, passion spent, he wanted to hold her and never let her go.

But Sara was already detaching herself from him, already arming herself against the hurt she believed would follow.

When he turned to say, 'I think we should talk,' she shook her head, knowing they shouldn't. Not now. Not when he might make promises that would later break her heart.

'At least stay for a while,' he said, catching her arm as she made to rise.

Sara felt she had little choice. She lay down again, and he drew her to him, kissing her gently on the lips. Then he cradled her head against his chest, his hand stroking her long dark hair, and, without meaning to, Sara fell asleep.

'What are you doing?' Neville asked, as he stirred from sleep to find her standing over her case.

Sara's heart sank. She'd woken earlier, with no regrets for the night past, but dread for the morning after and the meaningless conversation that would follow. For how else could it be, with her loving him and unable to say so, and him saying anything but the words she wanted to hear?

So she'd slipped out of his arms, and, taking trousers and sweater from her case, she'd gone quietly to the bathroom to wash and dress. She had hoped to escape before he awoke.

'What are you doing?' he repeated, although it must have been clear from the guilty look on her face.

'I have to go home, before my parents notice I'm not there,' she said as levelly as she could.

'I imagine they already have,' he replied, checking his watch to find it was past seven. 'How do you think they'll react?'

Sara answered with a shrug and carried on zipping up her case. Worrying about her parents was secondary to escaping from his room.

But if she thought Neville was just going to let her go, she'd misjudged him.

'Give me a couple of minutes to dress. We'll go together,' he said, rising to slip on his boxer shorts.

'What?' Sara rounded on him in horror. Was he crazy? If her father knew she'd stayed out all night, he was hardly going to welcome Neville for breakfast.

'Explain things,' he added, ignoring her look, and selected a pair of corduroys from his own case.

Sara turned away when he began to pull them on. He might not feel any embarrassment, dressing in front of her, but she did.

She waited until he was buttoning his shirt before she turned back. She found him smiling at her rather belated modesty, and she frowned.

'Explain what?' she pursued.

'Well, not the details. I think we'll rerun those on our own,' he said, his smile becoming sensual as he reached out to take her in his arms.

She backed away, with a sharp, 'Don't!'

It stopped him in his tracks, although he still didn't understand what was happening. 'What's wrong?' he asked point-blank.

'Nothing,' Sara lied. 'I just don't think it's a good idea your coming with me. You don't know my father. He's very old-fashioned.'

'You mean he's likely to take a shotgun to me.' Neville obviously regarded it as a joke.

'It's not impossible,' Sara warned.

'Then we'll have to see if we can pacify him,' he said, still in amused undertones. 'How do you think he'd react to the idea of our getting married?'

'Married?' Sara repeated the word as if its meaning eluded her.

'That's what I said.' He smiled at her confusion.

'You mean pretend to him,' she concluded slowly, 'that we're planning to marry?'

He gave a shrug, saying, 'Why pretend? We could always do it for real.'

Sure he must be joking, Sara snapped back, 'Oh, don't be ridiculous!' and went to pick up her case.

He caught her arm, making her stay, and this time any humour in his voice was forced. 'Well, at least you could spend a couple of minutes thinking about it. Or a couple of seconds even, for politeness's sake.'

'All right.' Sara held in an exasperated sigh. 'I'm sorry if I was rude, but I hardly think pacifying my father is a very good reason for marriage.'

'I do have others,' Neville claimed, sounding more than a little irritated himself.

'Really?' she challenged. 'Like what?'

'I'd have thought it was obvious,' he muttered back.

Doubting that his 'obvious' was the same as hers, Sara repeated, 'Like what?'

But Neville still hedged, 'Come on, you know how I feel.'

'I don't,' she stated truthfully.

'Or you don't want to,' he accused. 'Is that it?'

Sara shook her head, uncertain where the conversation was leading. She'd imagined him treating last night as casually as he treated everything else. It was that very casualness she'd sought to avoid. Now she was confronted with a belligerence that made little sense to her.

'Is that all I was to you?' he continued, his fingers tightening painfully on her arm. 'A little bit of relief, before you climb back into your widow's weeds?'

'No!' Sara was appalled. 'You can't think that!'

'Can't I?' he grated back. 'Then what was it all about? Tell me that!'

Sara couldn't, not without confessing how *she* felt. 'You wouldn't understand,' she said instead.

'Oh, no? Let's see, shall we?' he ran on angrily. 'If it wasn't just a one-night stand you were after, what else could I give you? Money?' he suggested, and didn't need her indignant look to tell him differently. 'No, of course not, your parents would be quite willing to give you that. So what else is there? What could a modern, independent woman possibly want from a man, without the complications of getting married?'

He paused, as if he expected some reply, but Sara was too shocked to offer one.

'Was that it, Sara?' he demanded, when she wouldn't meet his eyes. 'Was that what you were after from me— a baby?'

'Don't be stupid!' she said, trying to jerk her arm free.

But he pulled her closer, and with his other hand gripped her chin. 'Look at me, Sara, and tell me you can't be pregnant. Go on!'

Sara didn't need to tell him anything. Her guilty face revealed it all. She might not have schemed for a baby, but she'd done nothing to prevent one either.

'If I am, it's my business,' she finally muttered.

'Like hell it is!' he swore, and when she would have turned from him again he pushed her down on the bed. 'If you've used me——'

'I haven't!' she protested, as he stood over her. 'You're mad if you think I'd do that.'

'All right, maybe you didn't plan it.' He accepted the ring of truth in her voice. 'But it's still possible?'

'I suppose it is,' she conceded, before shaking her head at the absurd direction their argument had taken. 'Look, Neville, don't you think it's rather silly discussing some hypothetical baby I'm probably *not* expecting?'

His jaw tightened at her sarcasm. 'No, I don't,' he said stubbornly.

Sara wondered why he was reacting like this, so unlike the way she'd anticipated.

Then the parallel struck her. 'Listen, Neville, I can see you might be worried because of what happened with Annie and Scott——'

'It's hardly the same,' he interrupted, stealing her line.

'I realise that,' she responded. 'Judith Grant told me how much you cared for Annie.'

'What?' His brows lifted, as if this was news to him.

The gesture annoyed Sara. For once, couldn't he be honest about his feelings?

'Well, I wouldn't believe everything you hear,' he added carelessly.

And Sara lost her temper, demanding, 'Would it be so awful, if you admitted loving her?'

Neville was unmoved. 'Awful, no,' he responded, 'untrue, yes. Annie and I were friends, nothing more.'

He sounded so convincing Sara wondered if he was suffering from memory loss! 'So what about Scott?' she challenged. 'What was he? A *friendly* overture? Or maybe a divine conception?'

Anger made Sara sarcastic. She'd always hated the way he avoided acknowledging the boy.

For a moment he stared at her in apparent puzzlement, then his eyes widened as her meaning sunk in. 'I don't believe it! You think *I'm* Scott's father?'

The words 'of course' sprang to Sara's lips but were choked off by the incredulous look on his face.

'You do, don't you?' he prompted when she remained silent.

'I-I... Y-you told me you were,' Sara stammered back. 'The first night we met, remember...?'

She tailed off as she realised *she* didn't remember. Not once had he ever told her Scott was his son.

'But if you're not——?' The answer struck her before she'd even finished asking the question. If *he* wasn't Scott's father, then who else could it be?

'I take it the penny's dropped,' he drawled back.

She nodded. 'Your father.'

'The very same,' he confirmed.

Sara was appalled. 'Oh, God, I'm sorry, Neville, really sorry. The way I misjudged you... I don't know how to begin apologising——'

'Then don't,' Neville cut in. 'Let's just say we got our wires crossed.'

'But it was my fault,' Sara insisted, rising from the bed. 'I saw the resemblance and jumped to conclusions.'

'You're not the first.' He shrugged. 'When Annie was pregnant, I let her stay at my house for a while. I was partly responsible, you see. Not in the way you thought, but for introducing her to him.'

Sara, who had blamed him for so much, didn't see how he could blame himself for that. 'You couldn't have known what would happen.'

'Couldn't I?' His lips twisted in a grim smile. 'I'd spent twenty years watching my father with different women, convincing them and himself he was in love. I saw the look on his face when he met Annie. God, I knew his intentions before he did.' He laughed humourlessly. 'But I stood back and let him take her for a fool. He filled her head with all that nonsense about loving her and she believed every word.'

He shook his head at such naïveté, and Sara finally understood his feelings for Scott's mother. It wasn't love but a mixture of fondness, exasperation and despair.

Perhaps he felt something similar for his father as he went on, 'Not that *he* didn't mean it at the time. He always meant it...until the next one came along.'

'Is that what happened?' Sara asked quietly.

'Not this time, no,' he replied. 'When Annie told him she was pregnant, he actually asked my mother for a divorce. She duly refused it, of course, having remembered what a good Catholic she was. So, caught between a sobbing Annie and screaming Felice, he took the easy way out and had a fatal heart attack,' he relayed with his usual cynicism.

For once Sara found it understandable. His parents seemed to have spent their lives disillusioning him. Yet, from the way he'd treated Scott, he was a better person than either his selfish mother or father.

'Anyway, that's about it.' He dismissed further details as irrelevant. 'Now you know the truth, does it make a difference to us?'

Sara tried to convince herself that it did. It certainly made loving him that much easier now she knew *he* wasn't the father who had let Scott down. But how could their relationship last, when the love was so one-sided?

'I'm sorry, Neville.' Her soft brown eyes appealed for him to understand.

He clearly didn't, as he cursed bitterly, 'To hell with it, then,' and made to walk away.

Without thinking Sara reached a hand out to him, hearing the hurt in his voice, sharing it, and, when he turned back to her, she didn't try to hide the love she had for him.

But he still didn't understand, growling, 'Keep your damn pity, Sara Peters,' as he tore her fingers from his arm.

'It's not *pity*!' she cried back at him, no longer caring. 'I love you, you fool! Can't you see that?'

'You love me,' a stunned Neville repeated her impulsive words.

'Of course. What else?' Sara was suddenly very angry. 'Why did you think I slept with you? Out of pity? God, you're so stupid sometimes!' she declared furiously while he gaped in astonishment.

'*You* love *me*?' he repeated once more, the only thing he'd really heard, the only thing that mattered.

'Well, don't keep saying it!' Sara snapped. 'I can't help it. I know your rules—no promises, no commitments. Don't worry. I don't expect anything from you.'

'But——' Neville struggled to catch up with the workings of the female mind. 'But—if you love me...? I don't get it. I asked you to marry me and you threw it back in my face.'

'You were asking because you imagined I might be pregnant, that's why!' Sara accused, and drew another astonished stare.

'God, we're both fools!' he said, catching her face in his hands, forcing her to look at him. 'Don't you know I'm crazy about you? Don't you know I'd do anything for you, Sara Peters?'

Now it was Sara's turn to stare, to wonder how she could possibly have missed the love burning like a flame in his eyes.

'You've put me through hell,' he half laughed and half growled at her.

'Have I?' she echoed, not remembering things that way.

'Oh, yes,' he claimed, adding drily, 'Sometimes I used to think you went out with me just so you could crush my ego.'

'I don't seem to have succeeded,' she retorted, without thinking.

'There you go,' he threw back. 'You're still doing it.'

Sara realised he was right. Sniping at him seemed to be second nature. Perhaps it always would be.

'Don't worry,' he said, correctly reading her frown, 'I can live with it. I won't live without you.'

'Are you sure?' Sara wanted so much to believe, but she was scared to.

'I've never been so sure of anything else in my life.' He reached up and touched her cheek with a tenderness that made her want to cry. 'I thought love was self-deception until I met you, Sara. Now I look at you and my heart turns over. I touch you and the longing's so great, I can't even begin to express it.'

Sara felt the same. The idea of losing him terrified her. Yet she had to ask, 'What about other women, Neville?'

He didn't try to avoid the question. 'I won't lie. I've known more women than I care to remember. A few I've been fond of, none I've loved. I wanted sex without complications and that's what I got. But now I've discovered what real love is about, I can't imagine ever wanting to go back to that way of life,' he said with total conviction.

It was no guarantee, but it was as near one as Sara might wish for.

'Believe it,' he added quietly, and she realised he'd actually read her mind. 'I want to spend the rest of my life with you. I want to have children with you. I want to have a home full of love and laughter. That's all...' A smile recognised how much he asked for.

And Sara's answering smile told him she wanted the same—a life spent with *this* man, having his beautiful, dark-haired, blue-eyed children, giving them the sort of home he'd never had.

She thought then of Nick, and the life that might have been. But it was hard to picture. The memories were fading now. It was time to let go.

'What's wrong?' Neville asked, realising she'd gone away from him for a moment.

Sara shook her head, and said, 'I was just wondering the best way to break it to my family.'

'No problem,' Neville dismissed with his usual confidence regained. 'I got the impression your father would be in favour.'

'What?' Sara exclaimed, rapidly followed by, 'When?'

'Yesterday,' he revealed, 'when he showed me his collection. It was so obvious he was concerned about my intentions, so I assured him they were distinctly honourable... I wasn't to know yours weren't, of course,' he added in an amused drawl.

Sara made a face but couldn't really protest. After all, it *was* she who'd pursued him to his hotel room.

'What about Scott?' she said, changing the subject. 'He may not be too keen on having me around.'

'You must be joking.' Neville laughed back. 'The boy adores you. Ten years older, and he'd be the one proposing. As it is, he thinks you're too good for me... Which brings us back to your brother?' he finished with a questioning lift.

'Oh, he'll come round, I'm sure,' Sara replied, 'when we've been married a while.'

'Well, we will be,' Neville said, drawing her back into his arms. 'Because this is going to be for keeps, Sara Pet—Sara Dryden... Sounds good, doesn't it?'

'Mm,' Sara agreed, as he kissed her gently on the mouth.

She knew then it wasn't always going to be easy. But, oh, it was going to be worth it, she was suddenly certain.

All she wished for was a lifetime together. Laughing and fighting and loving, through the years.

my VALENTINE 1992

Celebrate the most romantic day of the year with
MY VALENTINE 1992—a sexy new collection of four
romantic stories written by our famous Temptation
authors:

GINA WILKINS
KRISTINE ROLOFSON
JOANN ROSS
VICKI LEWIS THOMPSON

My Valentine 1992—an exquisite escape into a romantic
and sensuous world.

 Harlequin Books

VAL-92-R

HARLEQUIN
PROUDLY PRESENTS
A DAZZLING NEW CONCEPT IN ROMANCE FICTION

One small town—twelve terrific love stories

Welcome to Tyler, Wisconsin—a town full of people
you'll enjoy getting to know, memorable friends and
unforgettable lovers, and a long-buried secret that
lurks beneath its serene surface....

JOIN US FOR A YEAR IN THE LIFE OF TYLER

Each book set in Tyler is a self-contained love story;
together, the twelve novels stitch the fabric of a
community.

LOSE YOUR HEART TO TYLER!

The excitement begins in March 1992, with
WHIRLWIND, by Nancy Martin. When lively, brash
Liza Baron arrives home unexpectedly, she moves
into the old family lodge, where the silent and
mysterious Cliff Forrester has been living in seclusion
for years....

WATCH FOR ALL TWELVE BOOKS
OF THE TYLER SERIES
Available wherever Harlequin books are sold